The Funeral Date

Carol Maloney Scott

The Funeral Date

Copyright 2024 © Carol Maloney Scott

This is a work of fiction. Names, characters, places, and incidents are products of the author's imagination or used fictitiously and are not to be construed as real. Any resemblance to actual events, locales, organizations, or persons, living or dead, is entirely coincidental.

All rights reserved. This book or any portion thereof may not be reproduced or used in any manner whatsoever without the express written permission of the publisher except for the use of brief quotations in a book review. For permission requests, please contact the publisher.

Formatting by Wild Seas Formatting (http://www.Rik Hall.com)

https://linktr.ee/cmscottauthor

Episode 1
Where Are the Leprechauns?

"Hello, I am Mrs. McNeill from Room 254, and I would like to know why are there no leprechauns in this hotel?"

The irate guest narrows her small mud-colored eyes at Tina the front desk clerk and I am counting to ten in my head hoping that I can resist the urge to jump in and tell her where she can stuff her leprechauns.

Normally as the hotel manager at the quaint boutique hotel, The O'Shaughnessy Inn, located on the beautiful Annapolis waterfront, I am patient and benevolent with my guests. Most of them are lovely people – parents visiting their children at the nearby Naval Academy, crab-eating enthusiasts, and history buffs.

But then the freaking month of March rolls around and the St. Patrick's Day revelers descend upon us in full force.

And this year we are even luckier because the holiday itself falls on a Friday. The Catholic Cardinal has lifted the "no meat on Friday during Lent" restriction so that all the hypocrites can eat corned beef with their green beer – so business is still booming.

Again, I'm not bitter but my boyfriend's parents shove their religious views down my throat on the regular and it's hard not to notice the inconsistencies.

For instance, we don't live together because they

would disown their son – in the year 2023!

But last night they were all blasted drunk and I was cornered by the creepiest of the creepy uncles, but I received more Irish blessings than I can count. I was rescued by Declan's father, but still...

Declan isn't like his parents but it's hard for him to go against them – he also works in the family business and unlike me, he started in upper management in the hotel chain after we both graduated from the top-rated hospitality management program at Michigan State University.

Yes, we met over the love of superior service and high thread count sheets, but I'd like to think our relationship means more than high profit margins and five-star travel reviews.

I'm slowly sliding away from the front desk, appearing to be engrossed in some plants that need watering in the lobby when Mrs. McNeill says, "I want happy, chubby little leprechauns – and instead there is a hairy man on the sidewalk wearing a green, sparkly fairy dress. That's sacrilegious!"

Tina closes her eyes for a moment and says, "Ma'am, I'm sorry but we don't provide holiday-themed entertainment here at the hotel."

I'm still tiptoeing away when our guest turns around and points her green polished nail at me and says, "Aren't you the manager? What are you going to do about all these disgusting leprechaun cross-dressers out there?"

I drop the magazines I was absentmindedly arranging on one of our marble tables and walk back to the front desk. Already there are a few people milling around from the bar and coming in from the street, and

I don't need a homophobic crazy lady upsetting the normal guests.

And yes, after last night's shenanigans, it's hard to believe there are any, but it only takes a few to push things over the edge. After all, not everyone threw up in the turnstile entry or in the elevator. And only a select few got arrested for indecent exposure by the ice machine.

I approach the woman and see that she's about my mother's age and maybe this is her first time traveling on this holiday weekend and she truly doesn't know what to expect.

Or how to talk to people.

Or how to be respectful of others' differences.

Oh hell, she's just a demanding, intolerant pain in the ass.

"Yes, Ma'am, I am the manager, and we aren't going to do anything about the people on the street. We don't control the city and if these people aren't breaking any laws then you should probably just ignore them. There's a bunch of cute traditional Irish pubs in town, and I am sure one of them will have entertainment to your liking."

She clutches her purse to her side and huffs. "This is the only true Irish hotel in town, and therefore you do control St. Patrick's Day here. You are the leaders of the community – I can't believe you would blaspheme on the day St. Patrick drove the snakes out of Ireland."

Just as I am about to reply, another guest wobbles up to the counter, clearly a little worse for wear from last night, or still hasn't been to sleep yet, and says, "Oh shut up, you old bat. You're putting my head off with your cackling – you've never even been to Ireland. My mum would never say…"

And the young lad is on the floor.

I forgot a whole bunch of Irish exchange students from the local university checked in last night and they've been instructing everyone on how to do things the Irish way.

I peer over the counter, "Is he all right down there?"

Mrs. McNeill says, "He's lying on my shoe. Get him off at once."

Tina rolls her eyes and walks around the desk, attempting to drag the delirious guy back to his feet, which is an impossible task.

"What is wrong with you people?"

Now Mrs. McNeill is trying to kick the guy with her sensible green pumps, and he yells out, "St. Patrick shoulda put all the snakes in your bed, you right old bi..."

And he's out again.

Now we have a full audience of spectators, including my boyfriend, Declan.

I'm sure his parents sent him over to see how things are going and I'm so glad he's here to help, even if he's also spying on me.

I suggested last night that I could probably use some backup this weekend, but he just laughed and joined in for the tenth rendition of Danny Boy with his creepy uncles.

"Addison, what is going on here?"

His blue eyes are slightly bloodshot and his thick blond hair is a bit messed up, but I can tell he still has his wits about him, as his mother would say.

My wits have left the building.

"Thank God you're here. This guest passed out on Mrs. McNeill's foot, and she is very irate that we don't have any proper leprechauns. I tried to explain to her that we aren't responsible for the drag queen show across the street..."

He grimaces and gets on his phone immediately. "Brian, grab Kevin and get down to the lobby. Yes, another drunk college student." He pauses a second and says, "I don't care if you dump them all on the sidewalk in front of the youth hostel. They are upsetting our guests and I want them out."

He shoves his phone back in his pocket and sidesteps the guy on the floor and says to Mrs. McNeill, "I am so sorry that our management didn't arrange for any entertainment this year. And I agree that what's on offer in town is quite inappropriate. After all, this is a holy day and all. I hear the Catholic Church two blocks down is running a lovely ceremony this evening. I'll have one of my men escort you after they clear out the undesirables. Please have a seat in the lounge and I'll let the bartender know to prepare you a nice soothing Irish coffee."

It's hard to be attracted to someone who talks like this to guests, but I've witnessed this sickening formal side of Declan in the past.

And I get it – he's only trying to placate the paying guests. I suppose I just don't want the money from people who ruin the vibe of the hotel for everyone else.

And the guy on the floor and his friends do need some tough love, but they are also paying guests. I saw plenty of bad behavior from wealthier, older clientele last night and they aren't being forcibly removed by Declan's big, dumb cousins.

As Brian and Kevin approach to deal with the mess, Declan says, "Tina, please go back to the front desk, and

Addison, can I have a word with you privately?"

Oh no, he better not be ready to lecture me on guest relations. When has his ass had to deal with these loonies?

As I swallow my temper and follow him to the office, I catch the eye of a cute guy sitting on one of the couches in the lobby, enjoying the show.

He looks vaguely familiar, but I am not sure why he's smiling at me.

Maybe I did provide some in-house entertainment after all.

Episode 2
Enough is Enough

"Are you kidding me right now?"

I know everyone at the front desk and all the way to the lobby can hear me shouting, but do I care?

No, I do not.

Declan just dropped a major bullshit bomb on me, and I can't believe my ears.

"Addison, no I'm not kidding. My parents just don't think this job is a good fit for you and they are willing to help you find something else."

He's sitting in the guest chair in the small hotel office, and I am pacing around the ten-by-ten space like a mad woman.

It's not enough space for rage pacing unless you're a mouse.

That's a good idea – I'll spread a rumor to the health department that there are mice in the kitchen.

I grit my teeth and lean back against my desk with my arms folded across my chest. Declan is forced to back his chair up to the door to get away from me and reclaim his personal space. This has effectively trapped him even more because the only exit is blocked.

"Your *parents* don't think so, or *you* don't think so? It seems to me that since they put you in charge it would be your call."

I tap my foot while glaring at him.

He runs his hand through his already messy hair

and says, "Yes, I do agree with them. You're on edge all the time and you're snippy to the guests."

"Sometimes the guests are assholes! You know that from working in the service industry – oh wait, no you don't because you were instantly promoted to management via Francine O'Shaughnessy's womb!!"

Someone raps on the door and yells out, "Hey cuz, everything okay in there?"

Declan tries to stand up, but he has no move to make in the cramped quarters so he stays put and says, "Yeah Bri, it's okay. You and Kev can leave."

"Oh, I'm sure Tweedle Dee and Dum aren't going anywhere. They need to protect you, so *their* Mommy and Daddy don't get mad at them. After all, they need their beer and poker night money!"

Declan is wincing and says more quietly, "Addy..."

"Don't call me that. I can't believe you think I am going to continue to work here until you find someone else knowing that I am fired, and your parents are going to find me another job. I'm not a puppet on a string."

Now he's reaching forward and trying to take my hand, which is hard to do because both of them are tightly fisted.

"Addison, you didn't let me finish. They really want us to be able to concentrate on starting a family."

I blink several times and if my head could spin like the Exorcist girl, it would.

"A family? We don't even live together so your parents can live in a pretend La La Land where people our age don't have sex before marriage. They *do* know that's how families are made, right?"

Declan sighs and says, "I was hoping I could do this at a more romantic moment but if it's right here and now, so be it."

My eyes are bugging out of my head as I watch my Judas of a boyfriend get down on one knee while smacking the other one on the side of the desk.

This office is not meant for two people.

"What are you doing?"

"Addison Marie Lennox, will you do me the honor of being my wife?"

He opens a box displaying a blindingly shiny diamond and even though I had previously hoped for this moment for several years, I can't help but wonder why now and what's changed.

"Declan, I don't understand. I thought we weren't getting married because I'm not Catholic and someday you were going to either become enough of a man to stand up to your parents or I would leave you before my ovaries turn into raisinets. And I'm finding it doubly hard to believe you did the stand-up thing because you are firing me because of your family. So, explain this whole thing."

I wave my hands at the entire scene and realize that he's stuck and trying to get up to preserve what's left of his dignity.

He closes the box and places it on the desk, using the sturdy wooden surface as leverage to pry his legs out from under it.

I'm not helping. The imaginary mice can chew off his leg for all I care.

I go behind the desk to give him more space to maneuver because this could clearly take a while, and he finally pops up and flings himself back in the chair, rubbing his leg.

He looks up and says, "I very much want to marry

you, but I have to ask one small favor of you in order to smooth things over with my family."

"Didn't you just do that by firing me and asking me to stay until you replace me?"

He looks at the ground and then longingly at the door.

I lean forward from the other side of the desk and say, "There's *more*?"

"We thought...I thought that you could enroll in the RICA program before we get married." He puts out his hand to stop me from saying anything and adds, "Just for show, you don't have to believe it. I don't care personally, but all the kids in the family go along with the traditions to keep the old people happy. It's not a big deal."

"The RICA classes? That better stand for the Regional Institute for Chocolate Addicts."

"No, it stands for the Rite of Christ..."

"Christian Initiation for Adults! You think I'm going to become Catholic to marry you? Are you fucking insane?"

Tina bangs on the door and yells out, "Hey, two old nuns just checked in – you better keep it down."

I hold my head in my hands. "Nuns...I can't...you're right, this is not the place for me. And just because I have red hair, half the nuts who stay here assume I'm Irish. And then others get Irish and Scottish confused and called me Lassie, like the dog."

"What are you doing?"

"What does it look like I'm doing? I'm leaving and I am not coming back. I'll send my sister for the stuff up in my hotel room...you know the only one we can have sex in because your parents don't know it's rented out to me?"

I grab my purse, jacket, and a few small photos and mementos from the desk and signal for Declan to make way for my final march out of this small, airless room.

"What about the ring? Addison, I love you."

He reaches out his arms and I place the ring box in his hand.

"No, you don't. I just make your life easy, and I am done doing that."

He moves out of the way and as I pry the door open, I say, "Oh, and I bet I know one tradition that you and your parents decided to forego?" I point to the ring box. "The one where the oldest son gives the grandmother's engagement ring to his intended. You bought that ring because there is no way in hell that Francine was giving her mother's rock to a Protestant. Am I right?"

Before he gets a chance to reply I practically fall over all the eavesdroppers on the other side of the door.

I can't blame Tina – she deserves to know what's going on because it affects her job, too, and she's my friend.

And Brian and Kevin can't do anything until they make sure the she-devil didn't hurt their fear*ful* leader.

Declan really is a wimp. He has nothing to say for himself of any note after I gave him eight freaking years of my life? And he's thirty years old and his parents are still making his decisions in 2023?

If it was a few hundred years ago they'd probably have me burned at the stake for heresy.

Brian peers behind me and says, "Declan, man, are you okay? How did the proposal go?"

Kevin punches his arm and says, "Shut up, you dickhead. Does it look like it went well?'

"I, for one, would say it didn't. Are you all right? Addison, is it? I couldn't help overhearing your name through the door."

The cute guy from the lobby has been standing at the door listening to this, too?

Does anyone have any control over the goings on in this hotel? Declan is right – I do need to let someone else run this place. I wonder if the nuns were invited to listen to our business too.

Declan points at the outsider and says, "Who the hell are you?"

"I'm Carter Lemieux and I would love to take this lady across the street for a drink. I hear they have fun people dressed in costumes and absolutely no nuns. And seeing as it seems her shift is over, she might be free."

He looks at me hopefully, and while I really just want to go home to my sister's townhouse and eat ice cream and yell obscenities, it would be a triumphant way to walk out this door for good.

"Actually, I think I will take you up on that offer."

I breeze past all the others and stand beside my new friend, Carter.

"See ya!"

I wave, and Carter and I walk to the door.

"You seem very familiar."

He smiles and says, "I'm your bourbon sales rep."

As I'm getting in the turnstile door, I hear Brian say, "This is bullshit. If she dumped you, I thought I'd have a chance with her next."

Yes, I think drag queens and a drink with the cute bourbon salesman are just what I need right now.

Episode 3
Family First

"You know, this place has been open for a couple of years and I've never been in here. It's a fun atmosphere."

My new friend Carter and I are lounging on one of the many couches in the drag queen bar across the street from The O'Shaughnessy.

My first thought was that we should find somewhere further away in case Declan or one of his dopey cousins decides to follow me, but no member of that clan is going to be caught dead here.

I am marked safe from homophobic O'Shaughnessy men.

Carter couldn't look more at ease in his perfectly fitting faded jeans and white button-down shirt with the sleeves rolled up. Men like him just love to show off their arms and I am all for it.

He takes a swig of his Guinness and says, "I stop in every once in a while when I'm in town. The bartenders at your place are okay, but overall, the crowd is pretty boring."

I nod my head in agreement even though they were not boring this weekend.

Now that I've made my dramatic exit from the Inn, I am at a loss for words. I don't know this guy, although since he said he's our bourbon rep I've probably seen him, or maybe even met him. The bar/dining manager meets with all the food and drink suppliers, but I know most of them.

And I don't think I would forget meeting Carter. I may have been in a "Declan-induced man haze," but my eyes still work.

With his dark hair and eyes, and the perfectly trimmed facial hair, he looks nothing like Declan.

I glance around the bar and can't help but laugh when I see the person Mrs. McNeill was so upset about. His makeup job is amazing – I should ask him for some tips. I must look quite plain in comparison. I have been rubbing my face in frustration most of the day and I am not wearing a single sequin.

I finally turn back to look at Carter and meet his eyes. "Thanks for getting me out of there. I probably would have stayed longer and there was no point."

"I just thought you looked like you needed a friend, but now I'm wondering if I shouldn't have interfered. I mean, maybe you and Declan should have gone somewhere private to talk things over. Have you been dating a long time?"

I sigh and pick up my hard cider. "Yeah, almost ten years. We met in college."

His eyes widen. "Ten years? Wow, that's a long time. Are you sure you don't want to go find him? He's probably cooled off by now. I thought he had asked you to marry him and it was like a "too soon" kind of thing, and scared you off. But ten years? Do you know how many women I've dated in the last ten years?" He winces and adds, "Never mind, that came out wrong. It's not that many, really."

I laugh and peek at my phone. I turn it over so I can't see the incoming messages. "No, it was more like too little too late."

I explain how Declan wanted me to become Catholic as a stipulation of marrying me and all about his controlling parents.

"Yeah, families can be like that. Mine is a little intense too, but they've always accepted the differences between me and my siblings. Honestly, the extended family has so many eccentricities they kind of have to accept diversity. Plus, the family businesses are pretty interesting."

I try not to show my distaste for meeting another guy who is working for a family business. I was thinking he was just the bourbon rep. But now I am probably about to find out he's the heir to the bourbon throne.

Not that it matters – I'm not thinking of dating a guy I just met after blowing up a ten-year relationship. Declan has been difficult for the past few years, and it should have ended years ago, but I still can't just turn off my feelings.

"So, your family makes bourbon. I don't drink hard liquor, but we sell a bunch of it at the Inn." I shift in my seat and say, "Have we ever met? I mean, Todd is the bar/dining manager, so I know he's your contact, but I feel like we must have met, unless we're a new account for you."

Carter smiles and I don't want to even talk about what that does to my insides. Also, my outsides.

"We met very briefly when I first took over the account. It was a couple of years ago. But you seemed very busy and frazzled. I will admit that I asked about you and Todd was very quick to let me know you were taken."

I feel a little bit of a blush hitting my cheeks and I'm glad it's dark in here.

"Oh, yeah, I'm sure everyone at The O'Shaughnessy made sure to keep men away from me. Maybe I would have met someone else if they weren't all so loyal to Declan and his family. It's like the Irish Mafia sometimes, but without the crime."

"Well, that's good to know. I'd hate to think those beefy Irishmen are armed and hunting me down."

"Haha, the only thing they are armed with is loyalty and stupidity."

We are momentarily distracted by a costume contest being awarded on the main stage. Not surprisingly the Irish man fairy won first prize, and the runner ups were a bottle of Guinness and a very sexy leprechaun. Too bad I don't know what room Mrs. McNeill is staying in off the top of my head. I could send him up to "entertain" her.

As we clap for the winners, Carter shakes his empty glass and points to the bar. "Do you want another?"

My cider is also drained. I do have to drive my car at some point, but if I really had to, I could sneak back into my room at the hotel or call my sister. She would pick me up absolutely any time and rescue me from any situation.

"Sure, why not?"

Carter heads up to the bar to refill our drinks and I take a moment to check my messages. Declan has sent several and each one is more annoying than the last one.

I should probably tell him that I'm safe, but he isn't worried about me. He is mostly concerned about looking like a fool. And if I know his priorities, he's searching for the receipt for that ring so he can get his money back.

Or maybe he'll save it for the next woman.

In some ways I do understand his family devotion. I

would kill or die for my sister, Erica. She's six years older than me but we were still close growing up. Even when she was a teenager, and I was an annoying little girl she still made time for me. And my parents are my rock. I guess I am lucky that I don't know what it's like to be pressured by family to conform to an agenda. My parents have always encouraged me and Erica to be our own women. If anything, I may have disappointed them by tying myself down to one guy so early in life.

Carter is back with the huge smile and the arms and the hair and all the other parts that are looking better and better as I am starting to realize that I wasn't as attached to Declan as I should have been.

I have not shed one tear, and I don't feel like I'm holding them back, either.

Carter places my drink on the table in front of the couch and sits at a close but respectful distance.

"So, Addison, where are you from originally?"

I start explaining that I'm from Detroit and that I went to Michigan State in Lansing, and then followed Declan back to Maryland after graduation.

My parents still live in Detroit, in a city neighborhood that has experienced a lot of gentrifications recently.

"You'd think that would be a good thing, but they aren't big fans of change. They liked their neighborhood the way it was. It was pretty safe, but like any big city, things have changed and I am glad that it's gotten a little more upscale. And they own a small house so it's not like their rent is going up, just their property values."

Carter tells me a little about growing up in Lexington, Kentucky on the family "compound" and how he still lives there.

"I moved out of the main house right after college, but we have so much property. So, I built a little house on the other side of the acreage. It's private and like I said, my family isn't interfering at all. Well, at least not in a bad way."

"Kentucky, huh? Isn't that horse country?"

I picture him on a big estate with green rolling hills on a horse playing polo. Although he doesn't look the part or act like the guy in my made-up rich guy fantasy.

Not that I would want to date a polo player who rides horses. I am allergic to horses. And there weren't a lot of animals growing up in the city, except the ones you call the exterminator to get rid of.

"Yes, Lexington is known for bourbon, horses, and basketball."

"Wow, I have no knowledge or interest in any of those things."

We laugh and clink glasses. I'm not sure why that's something to celebrate, but my guess is that Carter doesn't really care about any of that.

"I don't care about any of that. I rode a horse when I was growing up because they were there, and I do think they're nice animals. And I don't drink bourbon, either, except when I'm selling it. And then I can get away with a taste because I'm working."

"And what about basketball?" He's tall but not basketball tall.

"Oh, the university has a good team and it's popular with the locals because we don't have major league sports. I'll go to a game with my brother if we're both in town but otherwise I'm not a fanatic."

I'm about to ask him which sports he likes, thinking of all the O'Shaughnessys on Sunday watching football, when his phone rings.

He glances at it and says, "Oh, sorry, I need to get that."

I don't know how he's going to hear the caller in here, but I see the screen says "Mom".

I always answer the phone when my mom calls, but it is kind of late for a mother to be calling her adult son.

Maybe he is a mama's boy after all.

"Hi Mom, what's up?"

"What? I'm sorry it's hard to hear you. I'm at a bar. Who died?"

Episode 4
Time To Go Home

"Okay, Mom. Yes, I will come home in the morning."

Carter looks serious but not distraught, so I am assuming the deceased loved one isn't someone close, like his father. Whew...

I am trying not to openly eavesdrop but it's kind of impossible since he's sitting right next to me and practically yelling into the phone.

"No, I'll drive. Flying is a pain at the last minute to Lexington. I have my car on this trip. Yes, I'll be fine, Mom. Okay, I'll call you when I'm leaving in the morning. Love you, too."

He puts his phone in his pocket and says, "Hey, sorry about that."

"*What*? Why are you sorry? Someone died. Are you okay?"

He says, "Yeah, I'm fine. It was my Great Uncle Bernard. He is...was ninety-seven. He died in his sleep. He's my father's uncle. He and my grandfather were brothers. I'm sad to hear he passed but he lived a long, full life, and I saw him the last time I was home, which was a couple of weeks ago."

"Sure, it's always sad when someone dies but I guess at his age it's not a shock. And it's comforting that he died in his sleep, right?"

"Absolutely." Carter reaches over and squeezes my

knee. If he had done that before his mother's call, I may have thought he was being too forward. But I think now he just needs human connection. I would hug him, but it is awkward to hug someone on a couch without blending intimate body parts.

I don't have to worry about being tempted with any of that now, at least not until Carter's next visit to Annapolis.

"I'm sorry to cut our night short but I have to drive home tomorrow, and I should get some sleep. Also, I have to send some emails to clients to cancel a few things this coming week."

"Of course, no worries. Is there anything I can do to help? Are you staying at The O'Shaughnessy?"

I hope that didn't sound like I was planning on joining him.

And I just remembered that since I don't work there anymore, I can't do much to make his stay more comfortable.

I think I'll text Tina anyway and have her order him an early breakfast to be delivered to his room so he can get a good start in the morning.

He smiles and shakes his head. "I didn't even think about that. I don't know how welcome I will be there now."

"You're a paying guest and believe me, Declan and his cousins are not hanging out at the hotel waiting for me. Brian and Kevin are out partying, and Declan is looking for the engagement ring receipt or throwing the stuff in my room into the alley."

"Oh, that sucks. Is there anything valuable?"

I wave my hand and say, "No, just some toiletries and a change of clothes. We only used that room...never mind. I am texting Tina at the front desk to order breakfast for you for the morning. Eggs? Muffin basket for the road? Tea, coffee, juice?"

He gazes into my eyes and says, "That's really sweet of you. I eat anything so surprise me." He looks at his phone again and says, "I have multiple texts from my family members so I should get going. I really hate that long drive, though. Sometimes I fly on my work trips, but I love this area and I usually drive here so I have my own car to get around."

He stops talking abruptly and then starts again. He opens his mouth and then closes it again.

He looks like a guppy blowing bubbles in a fish tank.

"Did you want to ask me to help you with something else?"

I can't imagine what I could do but maybe he has decided he'd like to leave his car here. I could get the parking garage manager to keep it there until he returns if he wants to fly.

Before I get to offer, he says, "What if you came with me?"

I'm a little flustered but he really isn't giving off any creepy vibes. I could go back to the Inn with him, but I don't know about that.

"Oh okay, I could go back to the Inn with you. Like I said, I kind of would like to get my stuff. I don't have to come up to your room. We could find a place..."

"No, I mean come to Kentucky with me."

I blink my eyes several times and wrinkle my forehead.

"You want me to go home with you for a family funeral?"

"I know it sounds nuts, and I get that you might be

apprehensive because we just met. But I've been your bourbon rep for years. And I went to school with one of your employee's sisters."

I don't even know how to respond to this.

On the one hand, I can't drive alone in a car for like seven or eight hours to a strange guy's home. He could be a maniac. This could be a set up. How do I know that was his mom? Maybe he's a human trafficker and the bourbon thing is a façade.

Oh my God, there aren't any horses, I bet. He probably doesn't even live in Kentucky.

My sister would lose her mind if I did this. She works for Homeland Security, and I think her boyfriend is in the CIA, but they won't say or else they'd have to kill me.

What they *would* say is that I am the most gullible, naive woman on the planet to even consider this invitation.

But on the other hand, I just left my job, and my ex-boyfriend is not going to leave me alone easily. Even if just to appease his family, he will try to get me back.

And I might give in.

But Carter is a stranger, or at least a virtual stranger.

However, statistically most women are killed by their husbands or boyfriends. So, one could argue that I am safer with Carter than with Declan right now.

He is studying my face and I think he realizes that he's freaked me out.

"I'm sorry, I don't know where that came from. I know women have to be very careful and you really don't know me. We are just having such a nice time and I thought maybe you'd like to get out of town, too. You could stay with my sister or one of my cousins. Or my grandmother. She's ninety years old but she would smack me on the head with a bottle of our family's finest if she caught me sneaking into a woman's room uninvited."

"Um...that's good...I guess...I'm sure it would be perfectly safe and you seem very nice, but it's a family event. I wouldn't want to intrude on that."

He leans forward and says, "They would love it if I brought you, but really, I understand."

Just as I am about to politely decline and offer to order the funeral flowers or plant a tree in Uncle Bernard's name, I see a trio of idiots entering the bar.

He must have told his mother that I turned down his proposal and left with another man. For Declan to enter this bar, she must have told him to say three Hail Marys as Penance.

Carter follows my line of sight, takes my hand, and says, "Come on, let's get lost in the sea of people. I can get one of the owners to let us out through the drag queen dressing room."

That sounds like as good of a plan as any, so I allow myself to be led away from my past and towards...

"So, which one of my staff's sisters went to school with you?"

Episode 5
Should I Stay or Should I Go?

"Tina, they were so nice. They snuck us out the back door and we were giggling like little kids playing hide and go seek."

I am in the break room at the Inn with Tina updating her on the events of the past few hours while Carter goes up to his room to get his laptop.

She's standing up, leaning against one of the tables while I sit in a chair and wrestle with my current dilemma.

Tina is in her late forties and she's one of those middle-aged ladies that doesn't take any nonsense. She's worked at The O'Shaughnessy for twenty years, so she's not worried about helping me and making Declan mad.

As she puts it, "I used to babysit that little punk. I saw his underwear long before you did."

She smiles and says, "That's great but you can't hide from him forever. Maybe you should just talk to him. I'm not saying you should take him back, but the way you ran out of here - he's not going to let it go. But maybe you should lay low for a little while. If you go home, he probably won't bother you because Erica is scary, but she also works during the day. Now, I don't think Declan would hurt you or anything, but it's hard to get over a guy and think straight when he won't buzz off. Hey, I know - go on a vacation. Is there anyone you could visit for a while? Maybe your folks? Oh, but

Detroit in March is miserable. Hmm..."

She could keep on talking until Carter comes back, but I do value her wisdom, so I decide to tell her about Carter's invitation.

"He invited you to do what and where and *what*?"

She sits down and scrunches up her forehead and takes a deep breath.

"You know, my first instinct was to kill him when he gets down here, but you know what? It's not a bad idea."

"Seriously, you think I should do it? I was telling you in the hopes that you'd be the voice of reason and stop me."

Before she gets a chance to reply, Carter appears with his laptop and a quizzical expression.

"Hey, Tina. I'm checking out in the morning so you can give my room for tomorrow night to someone else if you need it."

I look back and forth between them.

"You know each other?"

Carter sits down and pops open his laptop. "I told you – I've been your bourbon rep for over two years, and I have been to this Inn many times. Tina works the front desk so, of course, I know her."

Tina gives Carter a side arm hug while standing and says, "Sorry about your uncle, kiddo. Safe travels tomorrow." Then she turns to me and says, "I can vouch for this guy, but you need to make your own decisions, Addison."

She leaves us alone and I say, "You went to school with Tina's sister? She's so much older than you."

He's typing and then looks up. "Oh no, I just know her from the front desk. I went to college with a woman named Gina, and her sister works as a sous chef in your kitchen."

"So, Sofia knows you, too? Does my whole staff know you?"

"Pretty much. I'm a likable guy." He smiles and goes back to typing. He looks even cuter while concentrating on sending his emails.

I'm starting to feel like he's not that much of a stranger if all these people here know him well, but now I'm wondering how many of the women he's "dated" were actually hookups with my staff in this Inn.

Not that it matters because I am not looking for a relationship or even a hookup. I just want to get out of town and not be murdered or sold as a sex slave, which is reasonable.

But how can I know for sure?

"Carter?"

"Hold on one second..." He keeps typing and reads his email aloud before sending it. "...and I will catch up with you on the first of next month on your order. Okay perfect, send." He closes his laptop. "I'm sorry, what did you ask me?"

I squirm in my seat and blurt out, "Can we call your mother back?"

"You want to talk to my mother?"

"Yes. No, well yes. I just want proof that you actually have a mother and that's where you're going. I know I'm accusing you of heinous crimes, but I just want to be safe if I decide to go with you."

He pulls out his phone and says, "Oh, you're still considering that? I thought no was no and I wasn't going to ask anymore. But sure, we can call my mother."

He starts scrolling to find her number and I realize

how late it is.

"Wait, it's almost midnight. She's probably asleep."

"No, she's still making phone calls and funeral arrangements at this hour. She takes this business very seriously."

He puts up a finger to say hold on a second while the phone rings.

I hope he plans on talking first because what do I say? "Hello, you don't know me but is your son really coming to your house and did Uncle Bernard really die? And are you sure you're not part of a human trafficking ring?"

"Hi, Mom, sorry to bug you...yeah that's what I figured...I wanted to see if it's okay if I bring a guest to stay with us for a few days." He's nodding and giving me the thumbs up. "Yes, she's very nice and she could use a break and...right...yes...no, just a friend...sure...okay hold on."

He puts the phone down and hits the speakerphone button.

"Okay Mom, you're on speakerphone. Mom, this is Addison. Meet my mother, Camille Dumas Lemieux."

He said that with a very authentic French accent.

The woman on the phone laughs and says, "Could you sound any more pretentious? Hello Addison. It's nice to meet you and you can call me Cammy. We are a family of French descent, but living in Kentucky for generations has kind of stripped us of French culture. So, I hear you're coming to visit. That's so lovely of you to keep Carter company on the long trip. He tends to fidget."

"Mom, you make it sound like she needs to bring my iPad so I can play some games and a blanket for my nap."

I smile and say, "I'm happy to come along, Mrs...I mean Cammy...but are you sure it's okay? Maybe it's not appropriate because of...oh I'm sorry for your loss."

Now my face is red, and I really feel stupid. If someone dies, that's what you lead off with in polite conversation – not your room reservation for your free vacation.

"Thank you, but we are going to be celebrating Bernard's life and legacy. He was a much-loved family member, but he was very old, and it was just his time. Now, let's talk about arrangements. I can put you in the lavender room. That's on the same floor as Carter's room when he stays with us, and I promise you I'm a very deep sleeper."

Now Carter looks embarrassed. How many women has he brought to previous family funerals and a game of musical rooms?

"Mom, can she stay with Scarlet, you think?" He turns to me and says, "Scarlet is my younger sister."

"Well, she's got a boyfriend now and her cottage on the property is very small. I mean, Addison can stay at your place. You don't have to stay at the main house."

Oh no, I need to take control.

"The lavender room sounds lovely. Isn't lavender soothing for sleep?"

Actually, I think that's the scent and not the color, but I'm anxious to solidify my spot.

"Okay, very good, I'll ask Caroline to make that up for you. Now you two get some sleep."

"Yeah, I know, Mom, next you'll be telling her I get cranky without my nap."

He takes his mother off speakerphone, and they talk

through a few more logistics.

It's done.

"Are you sure you're okay with this? You know my mother isn't encouraging me to sneak into your room, right? It's just her way of treating her kids like adults. I just hope you can deal with that room. It's like the purple palace in there."

Hmm...is that the usual funeral date's room? Has he spent a lot of time there?

"It will be great. Thanks for all of this. I do need to get away."

I sigh and take out my own phone.

"Then why do you still look anxiety ridden? I can call back and get you a room further away from me. I didn't even ask about Grandma Dominique. Or I'll just stay at my own place. I usually stay at the main house for family events, but I don't have to."

"The room is fine and I really appreciate it." I rub off what's left of my makeup to wake up for my next task. "The real fun begins now. I have to go home and get my stuff."

"And tell someone else you're going on this trip?"

"Yes, my sister."

I just hope he doesn't end up on the business end of her taser.

And yes, I mean that literally.

Episode 6
Sister Security

"License and registration, and while you're at it, social security number and will you submit to a lie detector test?"

Carter is busy emptying his wallet and replies, "What else do you need? Maybe the length of my..."

Erica's hand shoots up as imaginary flames shoot out of her ears.

At least she hasn't tried to taser him yet (although she has mentioned it as a possibility if things go south).

I called Erica to tell her what we were doing, and that we were on our way to pack my suitcase for a Kentucky funeral adventure.

I know what you're thinking – that idea would really take off as a guided vacation tour. Top seller!

Never mind touring the Scottish Highlands for the Outlander locations or Croatia to see where Game of Thrones was filmed.

No, this tour offers horses, a deceased old guy, and a yet-to-be-introduced cast of crazy relatives.

Also, plenty of bourbon, which may be needed.

On the way to Erica's townhouse, I learned a little about Cousin Caroline, who believes in crystal magic. She's making up the purple room for me, so I can't wait to see what she leaves under my pillow.

Hopefully, she doesn't also work with newts.

Then there is Aunt Violette, who is apparently

battling severe menopause and five-year-old twins.

She sounds fun.

He started to tell me about his younger brother Austin, who may or may not be trying to make meth in the horse barn because of course – he's a *Breaking Bad* fan.

I decided to hide any potentially felonious information from my sister. She's upset enough that Carter is a stranger, even though everyone at the Inn knows him and I spoke to his mother.

I tried to explain that many women go home with men they meet in bars and have sex with them, and all I'm doing is driving in a car in broad daylight to someone's parent's house.

Unfortunately, I then had to explain that no, I don't go home with strange men, and I'll be sleeping in the purple room, which is so far away from Carter's room that we would need a tunnel and a map to find each other.

Carter is taking this very good-naturedly and I don't understand why. I am an adult and if I want to go with him, I can go. And I just spent quite a while explaining to him how I don't like how Declan and his family controlled me, and now Erica is doing the same.

Erica says, "Okay the initial background check is clean. You don't even seem to have a parking ticket. I hate to say it, but I think we can avoid the lie detector. Let me call John so he can call off his guy."

While she calls her boyfriend, Carter looks at me and whispers, "Who *are* these people?"

I make the "shhh" expression with my lips. He doesn't want to know, and I am not even exactly sure.

Erica smiles now that she's gotten past the scary

portion of the evening and switches back into sister mode.

"Okay, sister dear, I am going to help you pack. I don't want to see any sexy underthings because we don't need them on this trip, right?'

I roll my eyes and follow her up the stairs. Carter is standing in the living room looking perplexed as he puts all his legal documents away.

Normally after this type of investigation a lawyer would appear to tell the suspect he's been bailed out of jail.

"I'll be up in a second, Erica."

I scurry back into the living room and say, "I'm so sorry about that."

Carter waves his hand and says, "It's fine. She just loves you and wants to protect you. I get it. Now go on and pack your stuff." He glances upstairs and whispers, "We can stop and get some sexy stuff at one of those shops along the interstate."

He laughs and I can't help but join him. Erica really is ridiculous, but even though I'm embarrassed, I also feel empowered. There is no way Carter is going to do anything I don't want on this trip.

For all he knows John is in the Middle East somewhere hanging out of a plane shooting at bad guys on a mission to thwart a coup.

You don't mess with people like that.

Carter sits down and busies himself on his phone while I join Erica upstairs before she has packed a chastity belt or some Amish outfits.

We pack my stuff in relative peace and harmony, and now she's telling me that Carter is cute and asking if I want her to "take care" of Declan.

Since I know she isn't asking if I want her to comfort him about the breakup, I politely decline her offer.

"Declan will be fine. Just please don't tell him where I went."

We laugh about that all the way down the stairs, as if Erica would tell anyone anything.

Needless to say, Declan stays away from my sister on a good day, so now I am sure he would not have the balls to darken her door.

He likes his balls just where they are.

After an additional grilling session about where we are sleeping tonight and what time we are leaving in the morning – "you better not fall asleep at the wheel!" – we are back in Carter's car.

"Whew, she's something else. Wow. I've never been so grateful for good city parking skills. Tickets would take on a new level of meaning if I had any."

I sigh and look out the window as we pull away from Erica's townhouse.

I call it "Erica's townhouse" because I just rent a room there and I am lucky because I pay very little rent and it's one of those new, schmancy places just outside of the historic district.

"I think she would have let parking tickets slide, but you probably would have to pay them as a toll for leaving town with me. Haha...but seriously, thanks for dealing with that. If you truly have no nefarious intentions, I don't understand why you would submit to that nonsense."

He turns towards the Inn and now I realize we have to talk about getting back inside undetected so we can stay there tonight.

"I like you, Addison. And yes, all of my intentions

are good, but that doesn't mean I don't want to get in line with all the other guys who will want to date you when you're over Declan."

He smiles and I must admit that he looks cuter as the night wears on. There is something about a disheveled handsome guy that gets me.

I want to say that I will most likely be over Declan in a couple of hours but then maybe it's a good idea to keep Carter at arm's length for a hot minute.

Erica is worried about my physical safety, but I know she is also concerned about me rebounding recklessly after abruptly turning down a public marriage proposal and ending a ten-year relationship.

I let a few moments too many pass before I reply, so I choose to ignore his last statement and move on to logistics.

"Okay, I need to text Tina and see if she can get us back in without Declan or any other O'Shaughnessys noticing, and I should ask her if there are any other rooms I can sleep in. If Declan wants to find me, he has two obvious choices – my room at the Inn or Erica's. Which would you choose?"

Carter's eyes widen and he says, "If Tina can't find you another room you can have mine and I'll sleep in my car."

He pauses and says with a smirk, "It would be interesting if Declan is forced to visit Erica tonight. I mean, I got to see her, and I wouldn't want him to miss out. What's fair is fair, am I right?"

Episode 7
On the Road

"We need to get gas. In my haste to vacate the premises of your former employer, I didn't notice I was almost on empty."

We're on the Interstate bright and early, having made it in and out of the Inn without seeing Declan or any others I wanted to avoid.

And Tina was able to find me a room – the one vacated by the drunk college kids had just been cleaned. It took the staff all day.

Fortunately, Carter didn't have to sleep in his car.

Although he would have noticed the gas.

He asks Siri for the nearest gas station, and I wait for her to reply with our choices before I say, "I can give you money for gas."

I reach down onto the floor for my crossbody purse, and he puts out his hand to stop me.

"That's very sweet but you are not paying for gas, or anything on this trip. I asked you to come and I would be making the trip regardless."

I purse my lips and say, "Okay, fine, but my parents taught me that you should always pay for gas on a trip if someone else is driving."

He signals to get off at the next exit and says, "I tell you what – while I'm pumping the gas go inside and get me some gum. I am a secret bubble gum addict. Not the grown-up kind – the little kid kind full of sugar."

I smile and agree to feed his addiction. I also need to make sure there's a bathroom so I can get that out of the way. I hate how often I have to go on road trips, but I'll just do what I always do and drink less. Declan was always so annoyed when I asked him to stop too often.

We pull up to the pump and both exit the car. Carter busies himself with the gas pumping and I head inside the small store.

I grab a bunch of gum – it's an eight-hour drive and I don't know how intense a gum addiction can get.

I also pick up some nuts, a bag of extremely unhealthy mini donuts, and a couple of bottles of water.

After paying and using the bathroom I meet Carter at the curb with the car running. He jumps out to open the door for me and I am startled.

"Hasn't anyone ever opened a car door for you? You looked frightened like I was coming over to attack."

We're both in the car now and while I'm putting on my seatbelt I say, "Well no, not really. I guess that's old-fashioned where I come from."

I put the water bottles in the cup holders and open both so it will be easier for Carter to drink his while driving. I used to open and hand Declan's drinks to him on a trip, but that seems a little too familiar for this journey.

"And here's the gum – should I only give you a little at a time?"

He grabs one pack out of my hand and says, "Good God, yes. Don't let me see all of that." He looks at the pack on his lap before merging back onto the highway.

"Actually, could you open a piece for me and pop it in my mouth?"

I guess I gave him an incredulous look because he

says, "What? I'm driving. I'll open my mouth really wide, and you can just throw it in."

I take the gum back and say, "But what if you don't clamp down on it in time and it goes down your throat? Then you'll be choking while driving." I look around the car for something I can use to hold the gum. "I know, I'll wrap it in a tissue, so I don't touch your mouth."

He laughs and says, "Addison, you can touch my mouth."

That seems unsanitary – I wouldn't want his fingers in my mouth.

Or would I?

"Okay, here goes."

I unwrap the big wad of gum and reach over across the seat while Carter's mouth is hanging open like he's going to get his tonsils checked with a tongue depressor.

"Okay, there, it's in."

Now, there is nothing sexy about putting gum in someone's mouth while driving in broad daylight.

But I still manage to feel a little jolt of electricity as my finger touches his lip and for a moment grazes his tongue.

I don't think he did that on purpose, though. Capturing that gum was a life-or-death situation. I can't give him the Heimlich and also drive the car.

"Thank you." He shifts in his seat and begins chomping.

I glance at his lap and notice that he looks a little squirmy. But no, there is no way that one little slip of the tongue...I was just feeding him gum. If anything, it's something a mother would do for a child.

I settle back into my seat and look at the time elapsed on the navigation app. Great, we have about thirty minutes down. Just another seven and a half hours to try to think of what to say or fight the urge to sleep.

I was also taught that it's rude to sleep while someone is driving. My parents always kept each other company on long trips, but I seriously doubt Carter is going to let me drive his car.

Now that I really think about it, Declan was a grump on long trips. Carter is over there smiling and popping bubbles.

Not that I'm comparing them because Carter is my new boyfriend. I've just been with one person for so long that I don't remember how other men behave in certain situations.

"Aside from enjoying my company and wearing black all week, what would you like to do in Lexington? It's a great town."

Carter doesn't seem to enjoy silence and I'm guessing he is going to lead the conversation if I let him. And why shouldn't I let him? My Granny taught me that you learn a lot more with your mouth shut and your ears open.

Just as I am thinking about what I might want to do, I say, "Wait a minute, what? I have to wear black all week? Isn't that something that only the royal family does? Or old Greek widows?"

He frowns and says, "I'm sorry, I guess we didn't have a lot of time to plan this trip. Yes, we wear black the whole week for all the funeral activities."

What is he talking about? What funeral activities? You go to a service and then the person is either buried in a cemetery or cremated, in which case it's over after the service.

Unless your Declan's family and the Irish wake is a

big thing, but even that doesn't last a week – just into the wee hours.

I really hope he's not going to tell me they play games or have photo shoots. I am not playing pin the tail on the casket or posing with a dead guy I didn't even know.

And what if I have to drink bourbon? Are there drinking games, like Shots for Uncle Bernard?

"Wow, that's…interesting…I only packed one black dress for the funeral. I don't think I've ever been to a multi-day funeral. I'm going to need to go shopping. Is there a Target in town?"

He glances at the navigation app which tells him to veer to the left and warns him about a police sighting up ahead.

"I'm sorry, what did you say? Target? Yeah, there's a Target. But there are so many nice boutiques in town. I'll have my sister, Scarlet, take you shopping. You'll like her. She's my most normal relative. And funny enough, she's going back to school to be a therapist. You know how the Mafia always sends at least one son to college to be a lawyer? Hahaha…"

How crazy are these people that they need to train their own in-house mental health professional?

He laughs and says, "Look at your face. I'm sorry, I'm teasing you too much. She really is going to school for counseling but not because of the family. She's just a nurturing soul."

I fidget in my seat and say, "I'm sure your sister is great, but I really can't afford to buy a bunch of expensive black clothes, especially now that I'm unemployed with no plan except to run away to a funeral with a man I just met."

Saying it out loud makes it sound pretty nuts. No wonder Erica initially flipped her lid and fired up her taser.

"Addison, I will pay for your clothes." I start to protest, and he says, "Really, I have plenty of money. It's not an issue, and it's my fault for not telling you what to pack. Although in my defense I was a little tense while the packing was happening. If I'd walked up the stairs to make a suggestion, I might have found myself at the bottom with a major head injury."

I sigh and say, "Okay, but I'm going to pay you back. And nothing too fancy. Hey, I know, maybe your sister has some clothes I can borrow."

He looks at me and says, "Oh, her clothes would never fit you."

I'm not sure how to take that so I change the subject, "Let's see what's on the radio before we get to West Virginia. Or do you have any good playlists on your phone? Wait, please don't say you like country music."

He laughs and starts singing something about a man and a truck and a horse accompanied by banjo twanging sounds. I can see the gum in his mouth and the sight of the pink blob along with the show is funny.

It's a lot better than thinking about my problems or talking about clothes. I know I'm not as thin as I used to be, so I am not going to attempt to squeeze into Scarlet's clothes. They probably cost a fortune and with my luck, I'll rip her pants open during one of the more vigorous funeral activities.

Episode 8
Home, Weird Home

"Oh no, I just realized I'm not wearing black now."

I look down at my jeans and pink sweater and realize that I'm going to start off on the wrong foot with these people.

"It's okay, you can change when you get there. You have the one black dress, right?"

I sigh and say, "Yes, but I was going to wear that to the funeral. I may have brought a black sweater – I honestly don't even know what I threw in the suitcase while my sister was giving me the code word to text her if I need to go to a safe house."

Carter blinks rapidly and smiles tentatively. "You're joking, right? You know what, don't even tell me. Here we are. Home, sweet home."

Before I get a chance to climb into the back and find something to wear in my suitcase, I notice that we have turned into a wide driveway lined by beautiful trees and flowers.

I wish I could tell you what kind they are since that would add to the mood of the scene, but I grew up in the city and I know more about garbage strikes and cockroaches than I do about crape myrtles and magnolias.

Those were good guesses, right? I do watch TV.

"Where is the house?"

"Oh, the driveway is a mile long, and I have to go

slow in case a little kid darts out of the magnolias."

See, I was right, although I still couldn't pick those trees out of a lineup.

I am thinking that I could hide in the thicket to change my top, but do I really want little Beauregard, the Third, telling Mommy that I'm the naked lady he saw in the bushes?

I can't wait to see the house at the end of such a spectacular...wow...

The Lemieux home is certainly gorgeous. It looks like a slightly smaller version of The White House, but prettier. If I knew anything about architecture, I could describe it more accurately, but it has enormous white columns, and the porch wraps around the whole house.

Honestly, I think this house might be bigger than The O'Shaughnessy.

I guess I am staring with my mouth hanging open because Carter leans towards me and says, "Hey, it's just a house. Don't go getting all weird about it." He grabs his wallet and water bottle and says, "Save that reaction for the people inside."

He's laughing again but now that I'm here I'm second-guessing my decision.

Well, I'm really probably at least fourth or fifth guessing it, but what is the worst thing that could happen?

If I don't want to stay, I am sure Carter would help me make arrangements to go home, and if they all turn out to be domestic terrorists or human traffickers, I always have the safe house code.

Carter comes around to open my door and collects our luggage as I gaze at the stately home. It makes sense that bourbon would be a lucrative business, and I'm sure the Lemieux family has old money.

And who knows what his mother's side of the family does for a living? They could be equally or even more successful.

We reach the front door, which looked very small from far away, but is massive and ornate up close.

Carter opens the door, and we almost collide with a woman in a flowing black dress with moon crescents embroidered all over it. It looks like something Morticia Addams would have worn, and I am half expecting Lurch to appear to take our bags.

The lady dressed as a witch is blond, mid-forties I would say, and smiling without her teeth.

"Carter, you made great time. And you must be Addison, right? Welcome to The Lemieux Estate."

Now that she's speaking, she is much less scary but still not what I was expecting. Oh wait, this must be the cousin...

Carter leans in and kisses her on the cheek, "Yes, this is Addison. Addison, this is my cousin, Caroline. You'll find she takes on a lady of the manor role when the family has guests. But with her, you never know if she is going to fluff your pillows or put a hex on you."

Caroline smacks Carter's arm and says, "Don't pay any attention to him. I just like to keep things organized and I don't put hexes on people." She turns to Carter and says, "We do need to find her something black to wear. I'm sure we have something with all the women in attendance here."

Unwilling to look like a charity case or cause any problems I say, "I have a black dress, if someone would just show me where to change."

She fans her fingers out on her chest in exasperation

and says, "Of course, my apologies. Carter is right. I do get a little obsessed with all the details. I just want you to feel comfortable. If it were up to me, we would wear bright colors at funerals as a celebration of life, but this family has its traditions. I will show you to your room. You're in the lavender room. It's got great feng shui and the vibe is to die for in there."

I swallow my words because I want to ask if anyone has ever died in there. This is an old house after all.

But as long as *I* don't die in there, I suppose it's fine.

"Caroline, where is my mother? I'd like to see her and introduce her to Addison before you drag her off to the other wing of the house."

How the hell big is this place? I wonder if Caroline's turn-down service comes with a map.

She lowers her voice this time and says, "Your mother is downstairs, so let's give her a few minutes."

Carter wrinkles his brow and says, "But isn't Uncle Bernard..."

"Oh yes, he's here."

She gestures towards the expansive open foyer and now I see him through the crowd of people milling around.

There is a casket set up on a platform like you would see at a funeral home.

What the hell is happening? The funeral is right now? And it's at the house? Did we go back in time?

People don't keep loved ones' bodies at home, do they?

That seems a bit...illegal.

But I've never planned a funeral or attended one in a mansion so...

And why is Mrs. Lemieux downstairs? Maybe they

have a chapel down there or something?

While I am trying not to look freaked out, a younger, shorter version of Carter sidles up beside me, wearing black jeans and a black button-down shirt. He's cradling a bottle of beer like it's contraband and the bourbon people will confiscate it if they catch him cheating with a rival alcohol.

"Well, hello, you must be my brother's latest funeral date. I'm Austin, the younger, better-looking, and much more fun one."

He is cute and seems more normal than Caroline, however, he lost me as soon as he called me the latest funeral date.

Austin is laughing and shaking his brother's hand and now they're doing the back-slapping thing men do.

"Little brother, can you please refrain from showing Addison your full personality before she gets past the foyer?" He turns to me and says, "I'm sorry but I really need to go say hello to my grandmother and elderly aunts and uncles. I'm sure they already know I'm here and they are getting ready to write me out of the Will. Caroline will show you to your room and Austin, please don't follow her. Remember the last time..."

"Yes, I'll behave. But in all fairness that chick liked me better than you." He does the finger-shooting thing and Carter shakes his head and walks away.

Caroline excuses herself to go find the keys to the "Pastel Wing" and I am standing here like a weirdo with Austin. But if I don't focus on him, my eyes might stray to the tuft of white hair I see sticking out of the...

Austin leans back against the front door and takes a swig of his beer. "I'm only joking with you. Carter's a good guy and I'm an ally here – trust me. Not that there will be enemies, but this family is...as the kids would say...a little extra."

"I'm sensing that...but in a good way..."

Austin is watching me watch Carter, who is now admiring Uncle Bernard with an old lady dressed in black lace.

"You're a little surprised that the casket is in the house, aren't you?"

While I'm glad he's addressed the dead guy...I mean elephant...in the room, I am not sure how to reply. I am not great at hiding my reactions, but I also don't want to insult these people and appear ungrateful for their hospitality.

After all, as my mother always says...it takes all kinds.

"Um, yes, I don't think I've seen that before, but I'm not upset about it or anything. I just didn't know if it was...you know..."

"Legal is the word I believe you're looking for?"

I am glad Austin and I seem to be on the same page. Maybe he *will* be my go-to person on this trip when I am not sure how to navigate these strange new waters.

I nod in assent to his questions, and he leans closer and says, "It's legal when your house is a mortuary."

Now I'm really wondering what Mrs. Lemieux is doing downstairs.

Episode 9
Horse Laundering

"Erica, I think this place might be a front for something."

I'm sitting on my purple bed in my very purple room in a house that doubles as a mortuary, trying to figure out where I went wrong with my impulsive decision-making.

"A front for what? I checked out the family and I didn't see anything suspicious. You know just because dead people freak you out it doesn't negate the fact that a mortuary is a perfectly legitimate business."

I blow out my cheeks in exasperation and hear footsteps in the hall. But I'm sure they aren't headed my way.

Caroline showed me to my room right after Austin dropped the bomb, so I didn't get more information and as always, I turned to my sister.

Also, he could be joking – he was very smirky.

"I don't know – money laundering, illegal horse trading, moonshine."

I can picture Erica's eyes rolling through the phone. "One of those things is made up, and I really think you're overreacting. Wait a second, I'll look it up."

I hear her tapping on her keyboard and she says, "Okay, Dumas Family Funeral Services in Lexington, Kentucky has been in operation since 1912 and the family home is pictured on the website. Or at least I assume that's it – big white mansion – looks like it belongs in a civil war movie?"

I lean back on the fluffy purple pillows and look out the window at the wide green lawns and perfectly manicured flowers. It is hard to believe anything nefarious is going on here, but it's a shock. I thought the family sold bourbon.

Maybe they need the bourbon so they can tolerate preparing dead bodies for...or maybe they use the bourbon to you know...no, that's ridiculous. They have chemicals for that. I think.

"Yes, that's the house. I guess maybe in the old days it was normal to live in your place of business and it only seems creepy now?"

"Absolutely, and look it says here they have several locations in the metro area, so the house probably still has its legal business status so they can display Grandpa Bob in the parlor, but it's not where they really do business."

"Uncle Bernard, but yeah you're probably right."

I still hear footsteps again and now I hear people talking – it's Carter's voice – "Oh hello, Uncle Gaston, yes, it's great to be home. Of course, the circumstances... yes, I'll catch up with you downstairs... I'm just... uh... seeing if my guest is comfortable."

I hear another man murmuring as he walks away. I hate to be more suspicious than I already am, but I think Carter is eavesdropping outside my door.

Erica is talking and I am distracted. "I'm always right, and I'm glad I instilled in you a healthy fear of...many things...but I think you're safe. Remember, it's the living we need to fear, not the dead. Oh, that didn't come out right since you're in a big house full of strangers. Just make sure you lock your bedroom door and if you smell formaldehyde, I'd get out of there. I'm sure they have Uber in Kentucky."

"Don't worry, if I get a whiff of a dead body, I will steal a horse to vacate the premises if I have to."

We say goodbye and Erica wishes me luck with her usual offer to take down anyone who needs taking down, and I put my phone on the charger. I need to make sure my lifeline is ready at a moment's notice.

Why did this idea seem fun and daring last night, but now not so much?

I tiptoe to the door and open it fast as if Carter is leaning on it and I want to surprise him...uh oh...

Now Carter is sprawled out on the purple carpet (there are all different shades of purple in this room, and there is a little white here and there, but I swear the room is *very* purple).

"I would offer to help you up, but I doubt you were walking down the hall minding your own business and happened to get tired and fall asleep on my door."

He sits up rubbing his shoulder and says, "That's it exactly. You know it was a long trip."

I purse my lips and fold my arms across my chest.

"Hmm...it was, and I'd like to freshen up and find my black dress, so I blend with the family."

I shake my head and offer my hand. He takes it and it feels nice and strong, even though I am still super annoyed with him.

"Thanks, so I think we need to address the elephant in the room?"

That's the same saying I thought of when I asked Austin about the...deceased person in the room. Do we think alike? Or do they breed small elephants and there's one under my bed?

Who knows with these people?

He gestures to the loveseat and says, "Okay if I sit? You didn't partially saw through the legs on it, did you?"

"Holy crap, you were leaning on the door, that's not my fault!"

Carter holds his head – I hope he doesn't have a concussion – and says, "Inside voice, please. You could wake the dead...oh sorry, bad choice of words." He moves over to one corner of the loveseat and pats the spot next to him.

I relent and perch on the edge of the seat just in case I need to make a run for it.

"Austin told me that he told you that the house is also a mortuary, so I came up here to explain further and also to see if you were settled in.

When I got to the door, I heard you shrieking something about a front for horse laundering and then I heard Erica's name."

He smiles and runs his fingers through his hair, probably looking for the bump on his head. "You can't blame a man for eavesdropping when he hears suspicions about his family being offered to *Erica*. No one wants a SWAT team showing up at Uncle Bernie's send-off." He pauses and adds, "Also, what is horse laundering?"

I lean back in the cozy seat and rub my temples. "You know what I meant. Well, maybe not because I don't even know what I meant and that's not what I said. But anyway, I just got freaked out. I'm not used to your family's somewhat unorthodox funeral customs."

"It's my fault, I should have told you. I think I have PTSD from bringing home girls in my youth and my mother talking about dissecting bodies at the dinner table."

I jump up again. "What? She cuts open the bodies before she gets them ready for the coffin?"

"Oh God, I am really botching this explanation. I blame my head injury. Can I lie on your bed? Over the covers and I'll dangle my feet off the end. I can't bend down to take my shoes off."

I nod and he lumbers over to the bed and throws himself on it. I can't stand the sight of his feet dangling so I start taking off his shoes. This is oddly intimate, even for someone without a foot fetish. I must admit that I did imagine the remote possibility of Carter visiting my room and ending up in my bed, but the circumstances did not include discussions of corpse-dismemberment or sweaty feet.

So far, this free vacation is not going to get many stars on Yelp.

I sit down next to him with a semi-social distance between us and wait to find out if his mother is a descendant of Dr. Frankenstein.

He stares up at the ceiling with his hands folded on his chest, which is so corpse-like, but I decide not to mention it. After all, it runs in the family.

"My mother's family has been in the mortuary business for many years, even dating back to France before they came to America. So, she's very comfortable with it, and when she went to medical school, she decided to become a medical examiner. A coroner. She was the Chief Medical Examiner for Fayette County for about twenty years, and now she's retired and occasionally works in the family business, but Uncle Gaston, her brother, runs it."

It sounds so simple and rational now that I've calmed down enough to listen to the actual story.

Also, now I can't get the image of Gaston from Beauty and the Beast out of my head. And that song, oh my God.

"Wow, your mother's a doctor. My mother works in a hospital cafeteria."

He sits up slowly and says in a lower voice, "Doctors have to eat, so that's important work too. I don't want a hungry doctor cutting me open."

He notices my wince and says, "Sorry, we forget sometimes that other people's families aren't so blunt about these things, and Austin just uses it to amuse himself."

"With all the women you bring here, right?"

He leans forward and places his hand over mine. I stare at it for a moment, but I don't want him to think he's crossed a line and remove it. I like it there. He totally has the passport to cross this line, but he may need a special visa for more. We need to see how the week progresses.

My stomach loudly gurgling breaks the moment. "How embarrassing, but the car donuts and nuts are wearing off now. I hope we're not late for dinner. People are probably looking for us...well at least you. I need to find my..."

Now he's rubbing my hand and maybe I'm not as hungry as I thought.

A sharp and loud rap on the door interrupts what probably *should* be put on hold (quick rebounds are NOT good), but whoever it is has some powerful knuckles.

"Come in." I quickly scurry to my feet, but Carter doesn't seem as concerned about getting caught on my bed...or his body has seized up from his earlier date with the floor.

A pretty young woman swings open the door and announces, "Time to get downstairs, brother dear. The pickle queen has arrived."

Episode 10
The Pickle Queen

Carter's sister, Scarlet, is leading the way down the halls of the Pastel Wing, where my purple palace room is located, on our way back to the main area of the house to meet the pickle queen.

Now one would assume that I immediately asked the question that would be on anyone's mind – who and what is a pickle queen?

Assuming I didn't just step into a young adult fantasy book, I am sure there is a reasonable explanation for this person's nickname, and I won't have to curtsy or kiss her baby gherkin ring so she doesn't turn me into a cucumber.

I decided not to ask for more information because I'll find out in a moment, and regardless of the answer, I can't run screaming back to my room. That would be rude, and I'm starving. But I am still not wearing the damn black dress. I hope I can find my room, or I may starve to death before I even get to the Horse Stable Wing or the Family Jewels Wing.

I made those up, but who knows?

As we are following Scarlet to greet her majesty and the others, I now understand why none of her clothes would fit me.

I thought she would be a teeny, tiny waif-like woman.

Nothing could be further from the truth, but it's not

like she's fat either.

She has a small waist and large, but normal-sized boobs. Her stomach is flat in her tight jersey-knit black knee-length dress.

Her legs are shapely, but the real showstopper is her butt.

She could easily have appeared in the old music video for Baby's Got Back.

Her butt is ginormous, but not in a bad way. It looks like you could bounce a quarter off it, but for multiple reasons, I don't want to get caught gawking at it.

Too late – Carter opens his eyes super wide in mock horror at his sister's back end and he mouths, "I told you."

She takes the term "curvy" to a new level and now I'm wondering where this exaggerated feature originated on the family tree.

For his sake as well as mine, I hope it isn't Uncle Gaston the mortician.

Not a good look on a man.

"Whew, I don't know why they put you in the East Bumblefuck Wing, Addison. Jeez, it's a long walk back to the viewing room." Scarlet is holding her long, wavy brown hair off her neck and fanning herself.

Moving that butt must expend a lot of energy.

Wait, please tell me she didn't just call their living room the "viewing room." Maybe that's what it is, though, and there is a whole other living area with a TV and other things *living* people enjoy.

Carter says, "Almost there, Sis. You should do more cardio."

"Haha, you try doing cardio with this butt."

My face flushes and while I know she can't hear my

thoughts it's a weird coincidence.

No, I am absolutely not going to entertain the idea that Scarlet can read minds. I've already worried about enough fears coming true on this trip.

As long as Uncle Bernard and his spirit stay in the box until whenever this insanity... I mean lovely tribute... is over, I can roll with everything else.

Scarlet stops just short of the hallway that leads us back to where we originally entered this dwelling and says, "Addison, Carter texted me earlier and said you only have one black outfit with you. Maybe you can go up and change after this, and I'll take you out shopping tomorrow. I would do anything to get out of this house for a little while and I am guessing you will soon feel the same."

Carter rolls his eyes, and she says, "What? I'm going to do my thesis on this family's funeral rituals when I get my PhD – so much material at my fingertips."

"I'd love to go shopping and see the town. Thanks, Scarlet."

She waves her hand. "Don't mention it – we're using Carter's credit card, so I'll slip a few things in for myself. And what do you think about lobster and champagne for lunch? There's a place downtown that flies it in from Maine. Our only local food is fried chicken, and my ass doesn't need any more of that."

I smile as Carter says, "You ladies get whatever you want. I'd like to spend a little time with the horses and Addison is allergic."

She scrunches up her face in mock pain and says, "Ooohh, I wouldn't mention that until you're in the family for about five years. Maybe after your first born."

I don't bother correcting her because obviously,

everyone is going to think I'm Carter's girlfriend and I don't know why I imagined anything different.

I suppose his mother is the only one who knows the truth and she's not spilling the tea.

We are finally back in the foyer and Scarlet is scanning the room for the pickle queen. I don't see anyone dressed as a pickle, so that's encouraging.

She turns and grabs my hand and says, "Oh before I forget, you guys should come back to my place tonight after all the... you know... and escape the old people for a little while. Oh, and I love your hair – those red curls are stunning. You must tell me your secret."

Hmm... eight hours in a car and a little dry shampoo from Target after five hours of sleep. Follow me for more beauty tips.

Before Carter or I can get a word in I hear a squeal that sounds like a little piglet, and I turn around and see that it is coming from a little piglet.

Well, a short roundish woman with a roundish face and a belly as big as Scarlet's butt.

And a diamond ring on her left hand that could be used to demolish a brick patio.

I am hoping that she is pregnant and that the baby is not Carter's. Anything else would take the awkwardness of this trip to a whole new level.

Carter says, "Hello, Laura. You look great - about to pop soon, I see."

Laura reaches forward with her short arms and her tiny, swollen feet and grabs Carter in a bear hug... piglet hug?

It's still not clear if and/or why Laura is the pickle queen, but I'm just waiting for more information.

And dinner. So hungry...

Laura smacks his arm playfully and says, "Now Carter Alexander Lemieux, you know it's impolite to discuss an expectant mother's condition in public."

Carter turns to me and says, "Addison, this is Laura Parton Jennings, the famous pickle queen. Also, drama queen."

Now everyone is laughing, and Laura says, "I can't believe Carter hasn't told you about me. We were best friends growing up – inseparable, right Carter? The Bourbon Baron and the Pickle Princess were the King and Queen of the prom."

"Oh, I see. Well, it's nice to meet you, Laura. Did you get promoted to Queen?"

I should sideline the snark, but these people are falling right into it.

"Oh, bless your heart. Of course, when I got married, I was upgraded to queen. Hahaha... it's just a little fun we have with our names and family businesses. Didn't Carter tell you? My family owns Parton's Pickles. You must know of them, it's a household name."

I do know them, but she doesn't need to know that I leave the room when my father sits in front of the TV with a big smelly jar of her majesty's family jewels.

Also, I always thought they were owned by Dolly Parton, but I am not going to ask if there is any relation. I am assuming if there was, I would have heard about it by now.

"Yes, of course, I recognize the... pickles, and no, that hasn't come up in conversation..."

I am interrupted by Carter's phone ringing, which is apparently another impolite event in Laura's presence, based on her facial expression – the same one I make when I smell pickles.

I've known Carter for about 24 hours, but I don't see how this woman was his best friend.

And I am guessing they were more than friends. But at least there is a Mr. Pickle. Pickle King? Pickle Consort?

Or maybe he has his own food or beverage-themed family name, like the Duke of Donuts or the Earl of Egg Salad.

And I just remembered her brother is here and he's the Pickle Prince – I almost want to go back to talking about corpses.

Carter breaks my insane train of thought and says, "Sorry, I need to take this. Excuse me, ladies." He steps outside onto the front porch and leaves the three of us staring at each other with awkward smiles plastered on our faces.

Scarlet seems challenged with thinking of something to say to Laura, although I assume they've known each other all their lives as well.

She smiles and says, "Where's your husband and the whole brood of children? Is this number five?"

"Oh, you're so sassy, Scarlet. He's at home with the kids – they'll all be here tomorrow to pay their respects to dear Uncle Bernard. And this is number four. We're so blessed."

"So blessed."

Scarlet sounds like she would be blessed with some time away from her family, but I can see why this can be used as research. She should get college credit for this week, like an internship.

Carter comes back inside after wrapping up his call and looks at me.

"Your ex is not a happy man."

"Well, I could have told you that. Wait, why? That

wasn't him calling you, was it?"

Scarlet rubs her hands together like a movie villain and says, "Oooo... is there a love triangle? Now you guys *really* have to come over tonight. And Addison, you'll love my boyfriend, Tim. He has red hair too."

What is she talking about? It's funny when someone thinks they are the normal one in the family, but they haven't quite managed to escape the crazy.

Laura says, "Tim, now there's a cutie. But of course, looks alone don't make husband material. And what are you guys doing tonight? Oh, never mind, I'll be half asleep by dessert and Tyler promised he'd rub my swollen ankles while we watch *The Great British Baking Show*."

I guess Tyler is husband material.

I thought Declan might be, but now I just want to know if he's angry stalker material.

Episode 11
Dinner with the Muppets

"It's lovely to meet you, young lady. No one has told me anything about you, but I hope you enjoy your stay. Perhaps we can get acquainted over our after-dinner bourbon. You know, back in the day it was only the men who were invited into the library but now we are inclusive and the whole family imbibes together."

Claude Lemieux is an imposing figure in that way of successful older men but seems friendly enough.

Before I can open my mouth Carter blurts out, "Addison hates bourbon."

He seems to have developed a habit of introducing me and then stating my dislikes, which are unfortunately the great loves of the people I am meeting.

Like his father and sticky brown rocket fuel.

I mean, I can hold my breath and sip a bourbon if I have to. Or maybe I should say I'm on medication that doesn't mix with alcohol. But then his mother is a doctor and might take a professional interest.

Claude puffs out his chest and says, "Well that's all right. We have brandy? Whiskey? Port wine? How about some chocolate milk with a straw?"

He's smiling but his wife is not.

"Claude, for God's sake leave the girl alone. Not everyone drinks until their liver is pickled. Do you have any idea what a pickled liver looks like? Well, it looks like a pickle and pickles don't belong in the human body,

Claude."

As if on cue, a tall, good-looking guy about my age joins us and says, "Well some pickles do." He makes a mock gasping face and says, "Apologies, Mrs. L, I just couldn't resist."

Camille Lemieux laughs softly and blushes. A woman who cuts up dead people blushes. The world is truly a strange place.

He turns to me and says, "I'm Peter Parton, and by some stroke of luck I am seated next to you, Addison. You don't mind, do you, Carter?"

Peter Parton picked a peck of pickled peppers.

While I am trying to say that ten times fast in my head, Carter says, "Not at all, enjoy your dinner. Addison, we'll talk later about the... thing we need to talk about."

Smooth operator, this guy is.

What he's awkwardly referring to is the phone call he received right before I had to dash upstairs to change because the dinner bell rang.

Yes, they have an actual dinner bell, and it was loud. It could wake the dead – no, I didn't check on Uncle Bernard. I was too busy trying to find my room without the aid of a bomb-sniffing bloodhound.

When I got back downstairs everyone was moving into the dining room and Carter parted the crowd to take me aside and give me the basic rundown.

That was Tina on the phone, and she said that Declan was pissed – both pissed off and pissed drunk – and said he knows I'm in Kentucky and is working on finding the location.

It's not like he's going to send a bomb to our exact coordinates like in a spy movie, but I am concerned. I never thought he would try to track me down.

That was all the time we had to discuss the new problem because Carter wanted to introduce me to his parents. And he's going to do a general introduction at the table since we don't have time for me to meet everyone individually until bourbon hour.

I was hoping to fly under the radar a bit more, but maybe after these initial introductions, I'll just blend. After all, I'm not Carter's girlfriend and these people are focused on each other and their mourning schedule.

Now Peter leads me to my seat, and I am honestly grateful that I am about to eat. I have to make an effort not to wolf down half the table and eat like a lady.

Mrs. Lemieux clicks a glass, and everyone quiets down to listen to her welcome us to Uncle Bernard's funeral services, which tonight will include after-dinner "sharing" time and a movie.

This just keeps getting weirder and weirder. And is this before or after the bourbon hour? At this rate, I'll be falling asleep at Scarlet's cottage later.

I am eyeing all the serving plates on the table, and this looks like some unusual food – I was hoping for a chicken or a potato. I'd even eat broccoli. Not kale, though. Luckily, I have never experienced a kale level of hunger.

Mrs. Lemieux is still talking and now she is saying that tonight we are going to enjoy Uncle Bernard's favorite dishes in his memory.

Uh oh...

Peter smiles and leans over to whisper, "Not a fan of frog's legs and escargot? How about some pig's feet and foie gras?"

Oh my God, seriously? Goose liver, frog's legs, pig's

feet.

What, no arms or fingers?

"We also have a delicious Couilles de Mouton prepared by our French chef – what a treat!"

I look at Peter and say, "Please tell me that's chicken."

"No can do – that's mutton testicles."

Suddenly I don't feel so good, and I can't imagine what I am going to eat. Maybe I can survive on bread until we get to Scarlet's place. She might have a potato chip.

Peter is laughing at my reaction but he's probably not kidding. And now I need to adjust the expression on my face because Carter is introducing me to the table.

He called me his "friend," but I see lots of giggling and winking, especially amongst the older people.

I smile and wave to the group like a queen. Not a pickle queen, obviously, but maybe one day I'll graduate to that level. I'm sitting next to a prince so who knows?

Camille pops back up and says, "Oh and I almost forgot, we thought Laura's children were coming tonight so we made Uncle Bernard's guilty pleasures, corn dog nuggets, and mac and cheese."

Everyone laughs at the absurdity of eating such childish food, but Peter says, "Addison and I will be happy to take some of that off your hands." He elbows me and says, "Thank God for my sister's little beasts."

Laura gives him a playful stink eye and it's obvious that the Partons are part of this family. They are at a comfort level I can't imagine ever attaining, even if I did stick around.

Claude says, "But of course, and the chocolate milk is on its way. How about a bowl of gummy bears for dessert?"

Camille smacks her husband's arm and I notice he's already eating a frog's leg. All I can think of is Kermit and I may be sick.

Carter is sitting next to Laura and now Peter has picked up on my discovery.

"She totally orchestrated that. I saw her switching the name plates earlier, but I can't complain. As soon as I saw you, I was hoping that you and Carter weren't an item. Although I am wondering why you're here then. Only a girlfriend hoping for a ring would endure this dog and pony show. Or should I say, frog and pig show? Oh God, now we'll be thinking about Kermit and Miss Piggy."

Another mind reader? Or maybe we are all thinking the same things because these people are nuts and a few of us are sane.

I stab a corn dog nugget with my fork and say, "It's a whole story. I'm kind of escaping something. Someone."

"Sounds interesting. I'd love to hear about it over dinner."

"Well, I don't think this is the time or place to talk about it."

I am buttering a roll and I wish he would just let me get some food in my body before asking me questions. I wish Laura would have moved my nameplate to the bathroom so I could get some sustenance.

He smiles as he serves both of us a heaping portion of gooey, delicious mac and cheese. If the mac and cheese was talking to me, I'd pay attention but since it's mute and Peter keeps yammering away... wait... what did he say?

"I said I'd like to take you to dinner tomorrow night. Away from here. Carter won't mind, right? Since you're a friend on the lam from... someone."

I fidget in my seat and glance at Carter, who looks constipated talking to Laura.

I feel like the whole family will need medical attention after eating this dinner, but they probably regularly eat the extremities of Muppet characters.

"Dinner sounds great."

Especially after this meal.

Episode 12
Be Like Madison

"I don't think you have anything to worry about. You're surrounded by family... well, my family... but we are influential in this area. If Declan steps one foot on this property and causes any trouble, he will be arrested."

Carter and I are hiding in the kitchen sharing an after-hours chocolate milk. It's not my normal go-to after-dinner drink but since that's usually water, I think Claude had a good idea. This stuff is delicious.

"Well, thanks for that. I don't want my presence here to cause any trouble for your family, and I hope this situation doesn't jeopardize your business with The O'Shaughnessy."

Carter stands up and walks over to the massive white sink to rinse out his glass. "It's not like I am held to a sales quota. No one cares and believe me, there is no shortage of places to sell liquor. That's why we're so rich – booze and death are two recession-proof businesses."

I finish the rest of my little girl drink and wipe the milk mustache off my mouth. "I guess you're right. How did you avoid working on the mortuary side? Not that it isn't a good job but some people..."

He sits back down at the table and pulls his chair a little closer to mine. "That's simple. Men aren't groomed for mortician jobs the way they used to be."

"It's nice to have fair hiring practices but you're their son and I don't see Scarlet working on that side of the family business."

Scarlet is managing a small bed and breakfast the family owns near the university. They mostly host college students' parents and businesspeople who want an alternative to a hotel.

"Yeah, she dodged a bullet there, but in general there is a problem with men working in the industry."

He looks uncomfortable and I can't even imagine what he's going to tell me.

"You don't know do you?"

"No idea."

"One word. Necrophilia."

Thank God I am no longer drinking, or I'd be down to zero clean black outfits to wear.

"Seriously? There are *that many* men in the funeral business having sex with corpses that it's an industry *problem*?"

"Yep, look it up. Now of course they didn't think *I* was going to be a problem, but they gave me a choice and I am not a big science guy. I am much better at schmoozing in bars."

"But...your Uncle Gaston..."

Now my Beauty and the Beast imagery is ruined forever.

"He's fine and he doesn't even work with the bodies. Who knows, maybe my mom was a tiny bit worried about him."

He laughs and I am not sure if he's joking or not. Note to self – don't be dead around Uncle Gaston.

I met him briefly during the "sharing" time and he was pleasant enough but seemed pretty deep in the bourbon.

And I was also introduced to Grandma Dominique,

who is Camille's mother. So maybe her husband was suspicious since it was their business before... no, I have to stop thinking about this.

Dominique is ninety years old and told me that she hopes I can stick around for her funeral because it's going to be a "humdinger."

I am not sure if she's dying soon or if she just meant she has some great party-planning ideas for when the time comes.

She is Carter's only living grandparent on either side, and Great Uncle Bernard was the brother of Claude's deceased father. Everyone keeps saying that he was like a bonus grandparent because he never married or had children of his own.

Austin was there enjoying a bourbon or three, and Caroline looked tired and annoyed with her father, Gaston, for drinking so much. She said it messes up his chi and his aura is cloudy.

If she says so I believe her. She informed me that she left some crystals in my room to help with my chi and aura, and I said thank you because what else is there to say?

There is also an Aunt Violette, who is Claude's sister and is coming tomorrow with her five-year-old twins and husband. Her husband is older than five, obviously, but quite a bit younger than Violette. It sounds like she has her hands full at fifty with a young family and the cougar thing has backfired on her.

Scarlet rounded out the group in the library and the "sharing" portion of the evening was actually quite nice. We went around the room and each family member shared a nice memory about Uncle Bernard.

Claude talked about how he was the cool uncle

whenever his parents punished him as a little boy.

Everyone chuckled at that.

Camille told us how he taught her to play the piano, and Carter was grateful for his support in teaching him the family business.

Then it was Grandma Dominique's turn.

She tried to stand but was a bit wobbly, which can be normal for a ninety-year-old lady, but she didn't seem to be paying attention to the theme of the event and thought we were toasting someone instead of sharing about the deceased.

She said, "I raise a glass to Madison. She just sailed in here not knowing a soul and that takes guts. She wasn't worried – she just said, 'fuck it' So, let's all be like Madison and say 'fuck it' to everything... and by the way, that Bernie was an ass grabber. One time in the kitchen..."

And she was off the couch and on the ground.

Because she's ancient and no one wants to deal with a broken hip situation many people were on her in a second, first of all, her daughter, the doctor.

"Mama, her name is Addison, and we are not toasting people. How many bourbons have you had?"

Camille glared at her husband, and he shrugged. "Hey. She's *your* mother. I just sell the stuff. Let's get her up to her room, and by us, I mean you and Caroline, and we can get back to our sharing... oh never mind... as the old lady said, 'fuck it'."

He raised his glass and incredibly everyone in the room joined in repeating the toast with varied levels of enthusiasm.

Scarlet's head was buried in her hands, and she was texting – probably asking Tim to call her with a pretend emergency.

I'd like to know how he got out of this event – he's *really* dating a family member, not whatever the hell Madison is doing.

Since I am Madison, I can say she has no idea what she's doing.

After everyone had consumed as much bourbon as they could stomach on a belly full of sheep testicles, we moved into the movie room to watch a screening of the life and times of Uncle Bernard.

It was interesting how they had some very old home movies, and it was too bad Dominique missed them because she was in a lot of them after Carter's parents married and joined the two families.

Although I did notice Bernard checking out her ass in one video so there is probably some truth to the ass-grabbing accusations, but since he was on the bourbon side of the family, he only grabbed living asses.

We don't know about Dominique's husband... may he rest in peace of course.

Right after the movie Carter and I excused ourselves and found the only empty place in the house without a bed or a toilet – the kitchen.

Now Carter is cleaning my chocolate milk glass, and I am telling him that I am going to change into something more comfortable to go to his sister's cottage, and no it's not lingerie. That is creepy.

"Hey, I didn't bring it up, you did. Do you need help finding your room?"

I sigh and stretch my legs. "No, I know where it is now. If I'm not down in twenty minutes, it means I fell asleep on my bed and I'll see you tomorrow."

He looks disappointed and says, "Okay, I know

you're tired. But I would like you to come with me. You need to meet Tim – he has red hair, too."

I smile and try to find the energy to laugh. "Haha... I'll see you in a bit."

He's just standing there, and these are the times when I feel strange in his presence. We have known each other a ridiculously short time but it seems much longer.

I guess sharing personal drama will do that to people.

I almost want to hug him but then that could lead to more and that's not why I'm here.

I still don't know why I'm here, but I am hoping the longer I stay, the closer I will get to figuring it out.

Maybe I'll have more clarity when the funeral festivities are over and Uncle Bernard is buried. Cremated? Entombed? Mummified? Set out to sail on a burning raft?

I can't wait to find out.

Episode 13
The Good Sperm

"I don't know about you, but I was glad Peter took Laura home after dinner. She's gotten consistently more annoying since high school, but I noticed you seemed to be getting cozy with Peter?"

Scarlet and I are in the kitchen of her cute, cozy cottage and I am "helping" her get the snacks ready.

Really, I think she wanted to get me alone so she could give and receive some good gossip.

I am leaning against the counter and I'm so happy to see that none of her snacks involve body parts. I may leave Kentucky a vegetarian.

"She was okay, but Carter seemed relieved when she left. Oops, that sounded jealous and catty, didn't it? And that's so dumb because it's not like we're dating... or anything."

Scarlet reaches into the back of the freezer and pulls out a pack of Skinny Cow ice cream bars. "Do you want one, not that you need diet food, but it's my guilty pleasure."

I am happy to accept any food that I recognize.

She's already downed her first bite and says, "About that non-dating thing – I tried to get Mom or Carter to spill the story, but their lips are zipped. But now that Grandma Dominique blurted out your life motto, I am dying to know the story. And nice job avoiding the Peter question."

I lick some dripping vanilla ice cream and feel a slight brain freeze coming on. I could use that as an excuse for my diversionary tactics but really, I'm just tired and it's only day one.

"Sorry, I wasn't diverting. Also, that was never my life motto until yesterday, but she nailed it. And I did like Peter. We are going out for dinner tomorrow night."

Scarlet dabs her mouth with a napkin and drops her Skinny Cow wrapper in the trash. "Wow, he works even faster than he did in high school. You seem savvy but be careful with him. He's a smooth operator and before you know it, you're behind the horse barn with your underwear around... anyway, never mind that... that's just a rumor and nothing to do with me. So, before we go back into the living room, can you please explain why my brother brought you here and why he doesn't care that you were flirting with one of his least favorite people tonight?"

Huh... he likes Peter less than Laura? If no one likes the Partons, why are they welcomed as family? Maybe the Partons have something on the Lemieux family. I can't help but think back to my original list of possible crimes, only now I would include necrophilia and giving guests food poisoning.

Maybe the Partons are blackmailing them? Extorting? Entrapping? Exhuming?

Oh no, that last one goes with the corpse crimes.

Regardless of what it's called, there is some history here that is not of the warm and fuzzy nature.

I take a deep breath and begin to explain how I ended up here...in Kentucky...with Carter...in Scarlet's kitchen.

Her mouth is hanging open and she says, "You only

met Carter yesterday? Wow, Grandma was right. You are definitely the 'fuck it' girl. You'll have to tell me more tomorrow when we are out shopping away from prying ears and eyes."

She glances towards the living room and as if on cue Tim yells out, "Honey, do you need any more 'help' with those snacks? Come on out – you can talk about us tomorrow and we're hungry out here."

She tells him we're coming now, but she looks like she wanted to reply with an equally smart retort.

But in reality, we are doing exactly what he said. Although sadly we aren't talking about him – just Carter and Peter. I'll try to give him some equal time tomorrow and grill Scarlet about *their* relationship. I owe it to him as a fellow redhead to give him some attention.

And no, of course I'm not trying to avoid talking about the men in *my* life.

We cover the short distance back to the guys in a matter of seconds (no maps or compass needed to find your way around here) and I am so grateful I changed into very casual clothes. This is such a normal relaxed scene compared to earlier in the evening.

After our secret kitchen meeting, I left Carter and went to my room to change into leggings and a soft sweatshirt in bright blue and miraculously didn't fall asleep.

The trick is to avoid sitting on the bed.

All the other family members had long since adjourned to their rooms and I wasn't too concerned about the color choice of my clothes. It was dark and Uncle Bernard couldn't see me... I mean... well, he's dead so he couldn't see me anyway... at least I hope not.

What the hell am I saying? I really need some sleep

– I hope shopping with Scarlet doesn't have an early morning start time.

I also called the front desk at The O'Shaughnessy and luckily Tina answered. She said Declan was drunk and babbling about me and Carter, but she thinks he's all talk.

Of course, he would know I left town with Carter – it's pretty easy to deduce, even for Declan. I left with him, and I haven't come back.

And it would be relatively easy for him to find out more about Carter since we do business with him.

This is another reason why it was so important for us to go see Erica and explain. If I disappeared with Carter without telling her, Declan could have tricked her into thinking that Carter was the bad guy...

Wait a second... no, Erica is too smart for tricks, but she could have found us quickly, and for no good reason.

I'm just grateful that the mortuary business is in Camille's maiden name since it's the business that's tied to the house. The bourbon website has nothing to do with the family manor.

Now that we're all comfortable and eating normal snacks, I resist the urge to get too close to Carter. I am sitting on one small sofa with him, and Scarlet and Tim are on the other one.

It's just naturally what makes sense. I can't expect Tim and Carter to squeeze onto one couch with their knees banging together because I can't trust myself with getting too close to Carter.

That's why the date with Peter is a great diversion. I need to diversify and keep things light and breezy so I don't end up back in a relationship before I've even had time to process the last one.

I'll be gone from here before too long anyway, although I haven't had a moment to even consider where I might want to go.

Going back home to Erica's is just going backwards and if I want a fresh Declan-free start, I need just that... a fresh start.

And a job.

Luckily there are Inns and B&Bs to run all over the country and the world.

I'm munching a chip drenched in salsa when Scarlet says, "So Laura will be back tomorrow with Tyler and the kids, huh? I don't know why that's necessary. And Tyler always looks like he's constipated when he's here."

Wow, she has that effect on her own husband, too?

Tim is absentmindedly rubbing Scarlet's back and adds, "Maybe he's just like that all the time. Didn't you say he was weird in high school?"

"Not weird, just a little nerdy. And yeah, that's probably true. I've run into him in town and he's kind of a wet sock. Laura just married him because she couldn't get looks and charm, so she settled for stability and good sperm."

She laughs as she pokes Carter's foot across the coffee table with her own.

The siblings both seem to have the habit of putting their feet up right next to the food on the coffee table.

I bet Laura would be appalled by their manners.

Carter sits up straight and says, "If you're referring to me, I am very stable, and how do you know I don't have good sperm? It's never been purposely tested."

Tim hops up and says, "Okay, that's my cue to refill

the drinks before we start speculating about my sperm. I teach chemistry, not biology, and before you say it, no I don't like *Breaking Bad* and I have never made meth."

He's still smiling but Scarlet cringes as he leaves the room. "He's a little touchy about the meth thing. He wasn't thinking about the show's long-term impact on his profession when he picked his college major."

We all laugh but I've never watched the show and I am not even sure how a person would ingest meth, let alone make it.

Carter says, "Mom could probably sperm test all of the men in the family." He looks at my face and says, "I'm joking. I mean, I guess she could theoretically, but I promise we're not that weird. And besides, our parents aren't very concerned with grandchildren."

My eyes widen and I say, "Really? My mother constantly bemoans Erica's career and her lack of little feet to knit booties for."

I hesitate to comment on myself but decide to add, "And even though she wasn't always crazy about Declan... my... ex-boyfriend... she was secretly hoping I'd give him the big Irish family he wanted."

Everyone lets that go because Carter doesn't know how much Scarlet knows and Scarlet isn't done questioning me. Tim is back and he knows nothing.

He distributes drinks and says, "My money is on Austin being the surprise super-breeder."

"Austin, really? Does he work in the family business? He didn't seem very serious when I met him."

Scarlet says, "Austin is the least serious person I know. He's a video game YouTuber."

I wrinkle my forehead. "And that makes money?"

Tim leans back with his beer and puts his arm on the

back of the sofa. "You have no idea. He's raking it in. While I'm sitting in class avoiding Walter White references and waking kids up with a bullhorn, he's sleeping until noon and getting ready for his busy day."

"So, what does he actually *do*?" I am dumbfounded that this is a career. I could be making money from videos instead of dealing with Karen-like ladies asking to speak to the manager about leprechauns?

"He plays a game with other people, records it, edits the video, and loads it to his YouTube channel. He has like 500,000 subscribers. And when you get to that level on YouTube you make a boatload of bucks."

Scarlet is watching me process this information and says, "Maybe you are hanging out with the wrong Lemieux brother. Haha... where was Austin tonight anyway?"

Carter says, "Baby brother is out partying every chance he gets."

Tim adds, "Exactly, he's out partying while I'm grading papers." He looks at Scarlet adoringly and says, "But I don't need to party anymore, I have Scarlet at home. And have you seen her ass?"

Everyone laughs while she shakes it. Apparently, it's fine to mention Scarlet's butt but no one has brought up the similarities with her mother's and grandmother's rear ends. I see where she gets it now.

No wonder Grandma Dominique couldn't sit down properly. She rolled off the couch because she's permanently sitting on a beach ball.

Episode 14
Aunt Violette Drinks

"Hey, Scarlet, I'm sorry to hear about your... uncle, was it?"

A pretty blond woman about our age grabs Scarlet in a hug.

She appears to be the only employee working in the small boutique in downtown Lexington on a Monday morning.

Well, it's almost noon – I am so grateful that Scarlet isn't a morning person. I desperately needed sleep.

Although it took me a while to settle down after a fun time at her place... and Carter walking me to my room in the main house.

He's a gentleman, I give him that. I truly don't think he has any expectations of getting anything from me as a reward for whisking me away from my troubles.

Or maybe he's not attracted to me, which is fine. It will probably make things much easier.

He said good night and told me he would be busy this morning with work stuff, and that he'd see me later at the family funeral cookout.

Doesn't everyone have those for the whole extended family on a Monday afternoon?

While I'm reviewing the state of my crazy situation in my head, Scarlet is extricating herself from the shop clerk's embrace and assuring her that Uncle Bernard was very old, and it was his time.

I don't know why people must go on and on when they are offering condolences. It's so nosy, like they need to know how upset the family is and what kind of relationships they had.

I just want to get to the burial... or whatever ends this celebration of life and figure out what I want to do next.

It's virtually impossible to think straight with all these planned activities with a group of strangers who for some reason are treating me like family.

I suppose it could be worse and Carter's parents could have told him to send his stray woman to a hotel. He is surely not single because his family is running off his dates.

Well... they are nice but odd. If I was seriously considering him as a boyfriend, I might be more concerned.

Of course, Laura does seem to be a permanent fixture in his life, and even married and as pregnant as an overripe watermelon, she clearly has some kind of hold on him.

But that's not my problem – I am here to stock up on a wardrobe of black clothes to make it through the week with the Lemieuxs.

Now I'm shaking hands with the shop clerk, whose name is Eleanor, and she's showing me every black garment they have for sale, including nightgowns and bathing suits.

Really?

I can't help but raise my eyebrows and Scarlet touches my arm. "Don't worry, we don't have a funeral pajama party, although let's not even talk about that in a joking way. You never know what this family can conjure up when it comes to sending off our deceased loved ones."

"That's a relief." I smile and don't ask if there is a funeral family swim time. It is only March in Kentucky, but who knows with these people – they may have an indoor pool somewhere on the property.

I begin sorting through the pile of clothes for the ones I want to try on, and I notice that somehow Eleanor knows my size. I am an average size so not hard to guess, but people are weird here. I feel almost too taken care of – if that makes any sense.

"Your family is so good at planning funerals I'm surprised they don't offer that as part of the mortuary services, like a wedding planner."

Wow, that's another idea that should not be uttered out loud.

Eleanor grabs some garments and gestures towards the fitting rooms and says, "Oh, they do. Scarlet and Carter's Aunt Violette runs that service." She lowers her voice and adds, "She's their father's sister, so not on the Dumas side, but they gave her the job when the families were joined because she's an... alcoholic."

She whispers the last word but also annunciates it in an exaggerated way in case I was going deaf and needed to rely on reading lips to understand all the gossip.

I glance over at Scarlet who is scoping out the black shoes.

"I think you should try these on. Let's get you in the fitting room so we can have lunch."

She's smiling ear to ear, and I know she heard what Eleanor said – she was standing right there. It seems as though the Dumas/Lemieux family is very open with their private business.

As in, they don't have any private business.

Eleanor is forced to stop hovering over us because more customers have entered the shop, and Scarlet and I seize the opportunity to find the fitting rooms.

I hope I'm not expected to model all these clothes, like some weird funeral fashion show. I'm okay with honoring people's family traditions but not if the family is like *The Addams Family* or *The Munsters*.

"Okay, try some clothes on, and let's get the hell out of here. Isn't Eleanor too much? When it comes to my family, the people in this town have no filter. And my parents wonder why I am attracted to the mental health profession."

Scarlet perches on a purple velvet sofa while I sort the clothes in the fitting room into piles based on the type and occasion. It's a funeral week – it's not like I'm a widow in ancient times going into mourning until my own death.

Oh... I wonder if they do that. I guess once the week is over if there are any old ladies still wearing black, I will have my answer.

I am about to close the fitting room door, but look around for Eleanor and say, "Yeah, she's nosy all right. But is that true? Does your aunt really plan funerals like people plan weddings?"

Scarlet wrings her hands and sighs. "Yes, Aunt Violette is the definition of a hot mess, but not just because of her job... or drinking problem. You'll meet her this afternoon with her hot husband and the twins."

"Sounds great." I close the door and savor a few minutes of alone time. I like Scarlet – if it wasn't for her, I'd feel pretty alone here.

Although, if Carter didn't have a sister, maybe he

would be here with me now.

Or he wouldn't have brought me to Kentucky at all. Now that I think about it, he asked his mother if I could stay with Scarlet when we called her from The O'Shaughnessy.

This is starting to make more sense. He knew I'd have a friend here, so he wasn't worried about babysitting me or me thinking that I was a love interest for him.

I quickly try on a few outfits, and I eyeball a few more – I don't need to try on every single thing. I am a standard size and I am looking forward to lunch, where I can have a rare meal that I choose.

"How's it going in there?"

I wish that was Scarlet asking, but Eleanor is back.

"It's going great. I'll be out in a minute."

I hope she doesn't just walk in – her boundaries are flimsy with her mouth so maybe she also likes visual gossip.

I can hear her talking to the next customers – "Scarlet Lemieux brought this girl in to try on clothes... yes, definitely Carter's new woman... and you should have seen her boobs... not impressive at all."

I make sure everything is tucked in and prepare myself for the awkward moment when Scarlet is going to pay for all of this with Carter's credit card.

Unless he has a thing for rescuing damsels in distress, I don't see what he's getting out of this deal. We haven't spent much time together, he has not made any moves, and now I'm having dinner tonight with his childhood acquaintance, wearing a little black dress he paid for.

About that – I guess I should inform him of this

development. Laura surely knows by now, and if that's true, Eleanor may even know.

Eleanor's fake smile is bursting as she leads us to the checkout counter.

"So, I hear you're from Annapolis. I just love that cute little historic area on the water. I used to date a guy at the Naval Academy."

"Yes, it's a pretty town, but I'm not from there originally. I just live there."

Well, I sort of live there. I don't really live anywhere at the moment, which should be more of a concern than answering this silly woman's questions.

Also, who told her about me or where I'm from? It's only my second day here and my first time leaving the family manor.

I hope Declan doesn't know anyone who went to the Naval Academy, but I don't think he does. No one in his circle is smart enough for that.

As if reading my mind, Eleanor says, "Carter called earlier and asked me to accept his credit card for your purchases today. And he may have shared a little bit about your situation. That ex of yours sounds romantic. I wish someone would fire me and propose on the same day."

Scarlet starts helping Eleanor fold and bag my purchases. "Yes, well we don't all have the same goals, do we? We'd love to stay and chat, but we need to get some decent lunch in us before the family funeral cookout. Last night, we had Uncle Bernard's favorite French cuisine, but today his guilty culinary pleasures are on the menu."

I accept some bags to carry from Scarlet and thank Eleanor as we walk out to the sidewalk.

Guilty pleasures?

At least we're talking about food, right?

It sounds like children are invited to this event, so I don't think anyone is going to be licking whipped cream off anyone else, but if you asked me if any of this seemed normal a few days ago, I would think we were in the fantasy aisle of the bookstore.

No wonder Aunt Violette drinks.

Episode 15
Mr. Hottie McHottiepants

It's not warm enough for a cookout.

Also, this can only be loosely defined as a cookout.

We are outside, but March is a weird weather month in most parts of the country and Kentucky appears to be no exception. The late afternoon sun is the only thing keeping us from needing blankets... which I am sure someone (probably Caroline) is off gathering.

Then we will be a bunch of weirdos wearing black under black blankets on a dark patio eating... I don't know what. I have not summoned the courage to assess the food situation.

However, my nice normal chicken sandwich with a Caprese side salad is on its way out and I may need a little hit of something before dinner.

I don't know where Peter is taking me but I'm sure it's somewhere nice.

I'm wearing black jeans and a black sweatshirt, black socks, and black sneakers. I am obviously changing before dinner.

And no, my bra and underwear are not black because if I am asked to show those I am out of here. I'm sure some Uber driver would be willing to come to the crazy manor home to take me to the airport.

Hell, if it got bad enough my sister would send an extraction team.

After lunch, I went back to my room and read on my

Kindle, and texted Erica to let her know everything is fine.

Apparently, my parents were wondering why they hadn't heard from me lately, and Erica told them that Declan and I broke up.

I'm grateful that my parents are the type to give a grown child some space, but I will have to tell them what's going on eventually. I would just prefer to update them when the whole update doesn't involve spending the week with strangers at a mortuary/farm/distillery where everyone looks like a cat burglar.

At least not without being able to communicate the next step in the plan because there is no plan.

It's like a non-plan and those are the kind that worry parents.

And also the people with the non-plan. Like me.

But worrying isn't going to help me and I'm here now so I might as well enjoy what I can. I know Peter is coming to this event and I just saw Laura waddle... I mean walk... in with whom I assume are her husband and children.

How does she get her husband to go along with this insanity?

This isn't even her family, and they are all dressed in black.

I scan the lawn and see that finally, Carter has made an appearance.

He smiles at me across the patio and suddenly ducks behind a potted tree.

Oh, I see why – he spotted Laura.

I wonder why he's so keen to avoid her, well... except for the obvious reasons. Again, I don't get it, but apparently, they are still best friends since childhood.

He scurries around the perimeter of the patio, and Laura's back is turned while she is schmoozing Carter's parents and patting her belly.

"Hey, sorry I'm late. How was your day out shopping with my sister? I heard she was taking you to Eleanor's shop, so I called ahead."

His deep brown eyes are looking down at me, almost glistening in the twilight. He's smiling and I know he is pleased with himself and thinks he's doing a fabulous job of making my visit comfortable by sending his sister out to buy me clothes, but...

"Yeah, about that."

I fold my arms and shift my weight to my other hip. This does not make me taller or more imposing looking in any way, so I just blurt out, "Thanks for clothes and all, I'm set for funeral wear for life... but why did you tell Eleanor my life story?"

He has the decency to look sheepish and runs his fingers through his thick dark mane. I shouldn't be noticing these things or how they are attractive or enticing because I am annoyed with him.

"I'm sorry about that. I called to ask her to take my credit card from Scarlet and I ended up telling her how we met and why you're here. I didn't think it was a big deal, but I should have known she wouldn't keep her big mouth shut. She has a bit of a psycho obsession with my family."

I nod and wonder if that has anything to do with him. Maybe Laura isn't the only local nutjob who sees me as competition for the Bourbon Boy... no, that's wrong. Baron. Bourbon Baron.

"Anyway, she used to date a guy in Annapolis a long time ago... that's what you were upset about, right?

That she might have some connection to Declan?"

I am about to answer when our attention is drawn to a new commotion on the patio.

A middle-aged woman with a messy bun and a little boy hanging from each leg is screeching while a guy who looks like a model is holding a bag of toys and her overflowing purse.

"Get off me right now! Look, Laura's little brats are here – go play with them."

Carter winces and says, "That would be my Aunt Violette."

"Hmm... yes, I heard all about her today, too. I don't know, if I planned funeral events similar to this one for a living I'd go a bit nuts, too. Scarlet told me not only does Violette plan normal funeral services like any mortuary would, but she also designs funeral "experiences," and that is what your family is known for."

And wait for it... the best part is that they actually rent out the common areas of *this house* and estate for these events.

Maybe the bourbon helps everyone to cope... except for Violette who had to give it up.

I jump when I notice that Caroline has suddenly appeared beside me. Where did she come from? The black clothes are making everyone stealthy.

She whispers, "Why do you think I need crystals to stay centered?"

She's got a point, but I don't know if those rocks in the basket in my room would do any good unless we were allowed to throw them at people.

Carter shakes his head and says, "No, she's fine with the job. Everyone in our family can handle dead people and their families. She just can't handle motherhood at her age. She was in her forties when she met Jeremy, and he was like fifteen years younger than her. She thought she would never be a mother and I think being with a younger guy got her all wrapped up in the idea of it. Then she got pregnant. At forty-five. With twins."

Caroline touches my arm and says, "I'll be down by the pond clearing my chakras if you want to get away from this..." She waves her hand to encompass the full picture.

I hope Peter arrives soon. As much as I was enjoying making Carter squirm, and fantasizing about some possible ways we could make up, Peter is not part of this family and is free to come and go as he pleases. At least he can get me out of here.

Wait... am I assuming that everyone else is a funeral prisoner?

If I use my imagination, I can substitute all the black clothes for orange jumpsuits.

Now Claude is pulling his sister's children off her legs and handing them over to their father, who looks like he just came from a photo shoot for underwear, cologne, or a Ferrari.

I wave to Caroline and turn back to Carter. "I get it that the kids are a handful, well two handfuls, but she's married to Mr. Hottie McHottiepants, so her life can't be that bad."

Carter looks beyond me with an annoyed expression, and I hear Peter say, "Did I hear you call another man by a long, silly term of endearment right before our date?"

Episode 16
Flying Corndogs

Carter's eyes widen and he says, "You have a date with Peter. You've been here for like five minutes and you already have a date?"

Peter says, "Relax, bro, we're just having dinner. Someone needs to entertain this woman. You just brought her here on a whim and dropped her into the middle of Crazyville."

Carter blinks hard and takes a deep breath. "She's not a child who needs to be 'entertained' and my family is in the middle of a funeral. And you are not my brother."

I roll my eyes and say, "Hey guys, I'm right here – right freaking here. I can do whatever I want. Carter, we agreed that this wasn't a romantic trip, and I sense some major rivalry between you guys. Are you sure you're not brothers?"

Just as Carter prepares to launch his defense, what looks like several corn dogs come flying past my face and smack Carter right in the side of the head.

Carter curses under his breath and points at Peter's plate. "Did you just throw a corn dog at me?"

I hadn't even noticed that Peter was eating – aren't we going to dinner? That's the reason for all this drama, but the way he's holding his plate it's more like a prop to please his hosts. I strongly doubt he is loading up on corn dogs, macaroni and cheese, and what the hell is that

– gummy bears?

We had enough kids' food last night.

I wish I could have met Uncle Bernard – he's a study in contrasts for sure. Sheep testicles and sour patch kids? I can't wait to see what's on tomorrow's menu.

"No, I didn't throw a corn dog at you, asshole. It's your aunt's rotten kids."

Carter stretches to his full height and replies, "Colt and Cash are perfect angels compared to your sister's hellions. Look, Annabelle is only two years old and she's ripping the heads off the newly sprouted daffodils."

For a second, we all jump into adult mode, looking for her parents or any sane grown person who can stop her destruction – and who knows, is she young enough to think she can eat them? Although, unless they're poisonous they are probably healthier than any of the food at this... shit, there goes another corn dog... also is someone frying bologna? I'm going to be sick.

"Hey, Peter, Peter pickle eater, you want some more corn doggies?"

Colt and Cash are only about five years old but together they are like something out of a horror movie with their crazy eyes and corn dog-launching stances.

Scarlet needs to finish her studies quickly – marbles are rolling out of heads fast around here.

Speaking of heads, I'm not chastising someone's two-year-old and if this continues to escalate, one of these idiot men is going to get punched in the head in this insane parallel fight between the generations.

At least all the old men are sitting down drinking bourbon and ignoring everyone around them.

Hmm... I haven't seen Austin. Why does he get out of... damn it, now I just caught a bunch of gummy bears to the face and I think there's one in my ear.

"Okay, I have to meet a lady at a lake. She's washing chakras and I'm pretty sure whatever they are, mine are clogged up."

Peter and Carter continue to hurl insults while the kids litter the patio with crap food, while everyone else laughs and drinks bourbon – except Violette, she's rubbing her temples while Mr. Hottie McHottiepants rubs her feet.

Peter yells out, "Meet me at the car in a little while?" He looks so hopeful as he dodges something green. "Hey, not the bacon-wrapped pickles – those are good!"

Oh my God, if he smells like pickles on this date...

I nod my head because he is still my only hope to get out of here tonight and head to the lake... pond... puddle... whatever body of water Caroline uses to seek refuge.

She'd probably settle for a mop bucket in a pinch.

Uncle Bernard must be rolling over in his... oh that's right, he's still in the living room. At least I think so. I don't know the protocol for body placement for a week-long funeral.

One bright spot – at least no one has wheeled him out to the patio.

Episode 17
Caroline Knows Everything

It's getting dark now, and even though the property is well-lit, I'm not really sure how to find this water Caroline was telling me about.

I don't know what people did before cell phone lights – did they carry flashlights... or just stay home which is what I should have done.

And by home, I mean my room at Erica's, or maybe even my room at my parents' house.

I hear some music and chanting in the distance, so I assume I am about to find Caroline.

I hope this isn't a nude ceremony, but maybe I'm just being paranoid. I did just fish a gummy bear out of my ear and a couple out of my cleavage so this night could go any which way.

Okay, I see her now, just barely though, in her flowy black dress. She seems to own a lot of those.

I don't want to call out to her in case she's in the middle of a poem... chant... spell... mantra...

I try to make some noise, walking purposefully and clearing my throat.

"Addison, I heard you coming, and I was expecting you, so you don't have to be all weird about it."

She turns around and she and everything around her looks quite normal, so I smile and come forward. The pond is pretty and a little scary at the same time. Water at night always looks a little ominous to me, even though

I'm a good swimmer. But obviously, I am not getting in tonight – I almost need a coat over my sweatshirt now that the sun is setting.

"This is nice, I see why you like it down here. Things are insane back at the house."

She laughs and says, "If I had a dollar for every time someone has said that... I'd just have a lot of dollars. And honestly, I think that's part of what's wrong with this family. Too much money and not enough sense. Although I suppose I've profited from it."

I want to sit down but I've never been one to sit in the grass – too many creepy crawlies. It feels odd just standing here with Caroline, who is a virtual stranger, in the dark, staring at the water. She's not big on eye contact.

"How have you profited? Do you work in the family business, too?"

She turns and looks me in the eye. "Addison, I think you're the one."

Oh my God, the one for who? Carter? The family? Hopefully not her.

"Here, let's sit down."

From somewhere on her person, she produces a dark throw blanket embroidered with little sparkly moons, similar to the dress she was wearing when I arrived.

Maybe all her outfits come as blanket and dress sets, or maybe this is the dress. I'm so confused and if I concentrate on listening hard enough, I can hear people yelling up at the house. So much for celebrating Uncle Bernard's life. But who knows – maybe they all drove him nuts and he's glad to be rid of them.

Wouldn't it be funny if these rituals were his dying

requests and he set everyone up for his amusement?

Hmm... if so, well played, Uncle Bernard.

Caroline smooths out the blanket and I sit down. "What do you mean by I'm the one?"

"I know that sounds spooky but it's just the way I talk. I took a lot of drama classes, and I was in a coven for a while, so I really have the witch thing down, haha... anyway, I think you are the one for Carter."

I scrunch up my face. "I'm not sure how you can say that. Since we arrived here, we've barely spent any time together and we really don't even know each other. I just ended a long-term relationship and I'm going on a date with..."

"I know, the Pickle Prince. But that's all part of the plan."

"There's a plan? Who has a plan?"

Caroline smiles and says, "That's the mystery, isn't it? But let's get to the more practical part."

Well, that would be nice. You don't just drop these nutso bombshells on people in the dark without getting to the point.

Caroline says, "I sense that you are wondering about the relationship between Laura and Carter."

Now I feel squirmy like I'm in the hot seat. Have I been acting jealous? Was I rude to Laura? She wasn't exactly all warm and fuzzy with me.

"It is a bit odd. It sounds like they have been so close all their lives, but she married someone else, and Carter doesn't seem interested in spending much time with her. Did they date in high school?"

Caroline sighs and says, "No, they didn't but it's not just because she was chasing Carter and he wasn't interested. It's more than that."

Hmm... what more could there be? High school isn't that complicated. Unless... as I was suspecting the families have some kind of dirt on each other.

I lean forward as if anyone up at the house could hear me with all the racket going on, and there's no one here but the fish. "Are the bourbon and funeral businesses... like... fronts for the mob?"

Caroline purses her lips and then bursts out giggling.

I don't know what's so funny. I say, "What? I don't know, everything is so mysterious and makes zero sense."

Caroline regains her composure and hands me a black stone.

When she sees I am reluctant to take it she says, "It's black obsidian – good for grounding. Your energy is all over the place. Now where were we?"

I take the crystal and squeeze it in my palm. It could just be a nice cool, smooth stone... but I am open to possibilities.

Also, I am starving, and Peter needs to feed me. A nice cheeseburger would also be very grounding.

"Addison, Laura has always been in love with Carter, and he had been mostly oblivious to it until he turned sixteen."

"Oh, when they went to the prom, and they were voted King and Queen?"

"Exactly. That night was a bad one for Carter. He kissed Laura."

I sigh and wish she would get to the point. Did her kiss turn him into a newt? Oh my God, maybe Laura's a witch? Her kids certainly seem enchanted with something not so good.

"So, what happened?"

"He went home and told his mother and then it all came out."

My phone buzzes, and my heart is in my throat. So much for the grounding crystal. Peter is texting me because he's escaped the patio and is ready for dinner.

Caroline gestures towards my phone. "I'll get to the point so you can go. I can't believe I'm telling you this because so much of my lifestyle depends upon keeping this a secret, but I have seen Carter suffer for too long with this knowledge... and I think it's ruined his attempts at real relationships."

As much as I can't wait to eat, this may be the story I've been dying to hear.

I just hope it's not like the secrets Erica and her boyfriend keep – if they told me they'd have to kill me.

"Go ahead and text Peter and tell him you'll be there in a few minutes. It's a simple story about the bond between two families. Haven't you wondered why the Partons seem to be like family when no one gets along with them?"

While that seems to be the very definition of family, yes, I have wondered and now that I'm alone here in the woods with Caroline... do I even want to know?

Episode 18
Do The Math

Staring at the lake I wonder if anyone would even notice if I just didn't go back to the house at all.

Well, I'd have to sneak in to get my stuff, but everyone is on the patio and this family creates enough of their own diversion to allow for a simple escape to be executed.

Honestly, someone could be robbing the place right now, and no one would notice. The only one inside is Uncle Bernard and he's not any help.

Peter would notice if I didn't meet him for dinner, but he would probably assume that I decided to stay here with Carter, and Carter would think I ran off with Peter.

Caroline just unloaded a bombshell on me and then decided that she needed to bring her newly charged aura, or something like that, back to the party.

I don't blame her for wanting to encourage people to go home, and I guess her renewed positive energy will help her facilitate the evacuation without adding to the mayhem.

She squeezed my arm and asked me to join her here again tomorrow night for the New Moon Ritual.

Apparently, the new moon is a good time to set intentions.

I almost laughed when she said that because I don't know what I intend to do from one moment to the next lately.

She also didn't finish her whole story (as if what she *did* tell me wasn't enough – it was!) about the Partons and their relationship with the Lemieuxs. She said if I want to know more, I should ask Carter.

That's going to go over like a sheep's testicle on my dinner plate.

Although I did survive that.

However, I didn't come here to help Carter confront the truth about his family... why did I come here again? Too bad I can't ask the New Moon questions, like the Magic 8 ball.

I look out across the expansive yard, really, it's more like a field, and see two figures walking toward the house.

They aren't coming my way, as that would be on the other side of the property, so I'm not worrying about them seeing me or asking me what I'm doing out here in the dark staring at the water.

There are lots of reasons that behavior could be looked upon with concern, but even if they did see me from far away, they might just assume I'm Caroline.

She's the pond person.

I squint and I am sure that it's Austin walking across the grass – I guess his cottage must be on the property in that direction. This family owns a lot of land.

Wait... is that...?

My squinting capability is maxed out, but I know that voice. They are clearly not trying to hide, and why should they? They are two (presumably) single people enjoying an evening walk.

I just can't believe that Austin would be interested in Eleanor from the shop this morning. That's definitely her – I recognize her laugh. She does seem to be obsessed with this family, and Carter probably finds her annoying, so the baby brother is a fun alternative.

Not for me, obviously, but Eleanor seems a bit immature for our age.

My phone buzzes again, which makes me jump. I'm sure I am perfectly safe out here, but I am not often in the dark, alone, in an unfamiliar place.

I should go because it's not fair to keep Peter waiting... oh, great. It's not Peter.

Fucking Declan.

Nope, not today, Satan. That's going straight to voicemail.

I can't deal with him now.

And of course, he's followed it up with a text because nobody leaves or listens to voicemails in 2023.

"Addison, I know where you are! Just come home – I love you, and the hotel can't run without you. I was wrong. Also, you can tell the fucking bourbon guy he's fired. Irish people can get drunk on any liquor – we don't need his crap."

Oh Declan, so many lovely sentiments and threats all wrapped up in a nice bow.

If I know him, and I do, he is trying to save face with his family and he doesn't care about me at all. And he is supremely lazy, so if he's the one running the hotel in my absence they won't need to worry about bourbon or better leprechauns for next St. Patrick's Day – they won't be in business that long.

I shove my phone in my pocket, stand up straight and take a deep inhale of Kentucky night air. I don't want to inhale too hard, though, because the horse stables are out here someplace.

My stomach is yelling loudly now, and I text Peter

to tell him I'll meet him in the driveway in a few moments.

I don't even care that I'm not dressed for dinner – we can go someplace casual.

I feel like I owe it to Peter to put aside all I've learned tonight and focus on a nice meal with a new friend, but it's hard to forget Caroline's words.

I can see why the family protects Caroline, even though she's so different from the rest of them, and why they let her live here in the manor rent free.

What I don't fully comprehend is why she chose me to break her vow of secrecy.

Maybe she truly does see me as the one who can make Carter happy and help him to break the cycle he's stuck in when it comes to finding love.

Caroline is a good person, and I'm sure keeping this secret is messing with her chi, aura, and general mental health. It's not fair for Claude and Camille to expect her to carry this burden.

So, it seems that Peter and Laura Parton are Claude Lemieux's children.

Therefore, do the math – it's simple fractions.

The Lemieux and Parton kids are all half-siblings.

I could have happily gone through life without this information, but it is beginning to explain a lot.

According to Caroline, of the five children, Carter is the only one who knows the truth.

I had so many more questions, but Caroline ran off before I had the chance to ask them. She may have felt overwhelmed by her breach of trust and feared saying any more.

Does Camille know her husband fathered the children of their best family friends?

She must because Caroline said that Carter found out the truth after his mother learned that he kissed Laura at the prom. Did his mother tell him? Plant a clue?

Poor Carter, no wonder he's struggled with relationships.

And to add to it, for the past fourteen years since the prom, Laura has been a constant and flirtatious fixture in his life.

But if Camille knows, why would she continue to welcome the Partons into her home and life? They have their own mother.

At least I think they do.

Actually, where the hell are the Parton parents?

I sigh as the patio comes into view – I am going the long way around in the grass to reach the driveway. I've had enough craziness for one night and I just want to meet up with Peter and get the hell out of here.

And are Laura and Peter really in the dark about all of this? How could Caroline possibly know that for sure?

I thought my love life was messed up, but I am reasonably sure that I've never kissed my brother.

Episode 19
I Want a Secret

Violette and McHottiepants are getting in their car – well, she's in the car and he is holding the leg of one kid with each arm and attempting to toss them in the back seat.

It sounds much worse than it is – no children are being harmed, just the emotional state of parents.

Speaking of parents, I wonder if Laura and her brood have left yet, or if she's still latched onto Carter now that the crowd is thinning out.

Her poor husband... but seriously why would he marry a woman who clearly wants someone else she can't have... and then proceed to impregnate her multiple times?

Maybe the pickle fortune is just too good to pass up.

It seems like everyone has secrets now, except me.

I feel left out, and I want a secret, but I'd have to do something worthy of hiding.

I spot Peter standing by his car, shaking like a dog. What the hell?

He's looking at his phone and I call out, "Hey, Peter, is everything okay? Sorry, I kept you waiting. I was talking to Caroline at the... what the hell happened to you?"

He's soaking wet – why is he wet?

"Why are you wet?"

I don't recall seeing him at the pond, so I should stop

my crazy thoughts before they take hold. Obviously, he wasn't hiding near the pond eavesdropping on my conversation with Caroline and he fell in.

That would be ridiculous.

He tosses his phone into the car and climbs in rooting around in the back seat.

He pops back out with a towel with a giant smiling pickle on it and starts drying his hair.

Ooh, with all the product in his mane, it's probably going to dry crunchy, but I am not offering him a shampoo in my guest bath.

He huffs and says, "Those damn kids got out the super soakers and let loose. You'd think someone among the many adults present would have stopped that before it started, but finally, Tyler and Jeremy tackled the instigators and confiscated the weapons. Carter is soaked, too. Unbelievable."

"Who's Jeremy? Oh, you mean Hot... never mind... that's Violette's husband, and Tyler is your brother-in-law."

"More like wimp-in-law. And my sister and Violette aren't winning Mother of the Year."

I gulp as Peter takes off his black t-shirt and tosses it into the car with the pickle towel and his phone.

Caroline thinks I'm the one for Carter, but I don't know.

Peter is putting on a good show and he hasn't kissed his sister as far as I know. Although didn't Scarlet say something about Peter and behind the horse barn? But she could be talking in general, or about another girl they both knew.

Oh my God, I hope Scarlet and Peter have not swapped any body parts or fluids.

I sense all my potential new friendships going up in smoke.

Maybe I should just go home, face Declan and tell him to stay away from me. I'm sure Erica has a spare taser I could borrow, and there are lots of other hotels in Annapolis that would hire me.

Peter is taking his sweet, merry time putting on the new shirt he unearthed from his car, and I wonder if he's giving me a purposeful show of his abs and chest and all the other goodies on full display.

Honestly, why am I worried about who has done what with whom?

None of these people are *my* siblings.

My father isn't a perfect man (just ask my mother), but he hasn't impregnated any family friends.

Although, I am guessing that Scarlet and Austin probably think the same thing.

I can't worry about that now because once again my stomach is screaming at my brain to find some food or it's going to cut off all thinking capabilities.

"Okay, that's better. And I'm finally not wearing black."

He glances down at the snug burnt orange shirt he's now sporting. It's picking up a glint of gold in his brown eyes reflected in the driveway lights, which I now realize are also Carter's eyes.

Damn it.

I smile and look down at my own rather hideous outfit and he says, "Did you want to change? You don't have to – we can go somewhere casual if you want, but no corn dogs."

"Yeah, I'm good to go like this, and as long as we aren't going to an elementary school cafeteria, I think we're safe from corn dogs."

"Okay, but I do have a bunch of shirts in the car you could wear?"

What an odd thing to say. Is this a car or a closet? Also, if he thinks I am changing my shirt in the driveway he's nuts.

However, that could start me on a path to becoming a person with secrets.

Okay, it would be a tame and lame start, but either way – my boobs are staying behind the black sweatshirt veil for now.

I haven't figured out if I am interested in Peter... or Carter... or no one.

I could just get a cute little dog and take up a hobby, like piano lessons. And avoid this whole marriage and family thing forever – the examples I've seen here are certainly not good advertisements.

"Haha... no, I'm good... I was at the pond with Caroline, but she didn't attack me with any water. I'm nice and dry... and starving. How about burgers?"

I need meat, but fortunately, I didn't say that out loud.

Episode 20
Pickle Infidelity

Peter is still trying to dry and restyle his hair with his fingers every time we stop at a light before finally turning into a bright shopping center and parking in front of a fun-looking burger place.

This is just what I need – some normalcy.

I bend down to grab my purse and when I look up Peter is wearing sunglasses and a University of Kentucky baseball cap.

My puzzled expression prompts him to say, "This is my favorite burger place in town, but I can't be recognized here."

What the hell – when does the insanity end?

"Okay, I'll bite. Why can't you be recognized? Crazy ex works here?"

I can't think of any other reasons – I doubt Peter got drunk and disorderly or left without paying his bill.

"It's the pickles."

"The pickles?"

"They don't use Parton's Pickles on their burgers. So, because they refuse to buy from us and use a competitor's pickles, they are the enemy."

I open my mouth into an exaggerated "O" shape. "Well, that makes perfect sense. The pickle wars, naturally."

"Make fun all you want but if my parents knew I was here..."

He shakes his head at the supposed horrors his parents would bestow upon him if they knew of his pickle infidelity.

Never mind the fact that his father isn't his father and apparently no one has bothered to tell him that fact. If ever there was a case of the wrong "pickle" going... anyway, what is he saying now? Oh, his parents... I do want to hear more about them.

As we get out of the car and walk to the restaurant, he tells me how his parents have been on a world cruise for the past three months and they are due home soon.

"Of course, they would be here for Bernard's funeral, but they just couldn't get back. They never miss a Lemieux family function and I know they're missing their best friends."

Hmm... their best friends? What about their children and grandchildren – their daughter looks ready to pop any day now.

As we are seated, I am so glad that we didn't go to a fancy restaurant. It's not that I'm not used to nice things – dating Declan did expose me to a lot more wealth than I had growing up, and Erica is doing very well also, but I am just tired of all the rules and norms of Carter's family.

Although I am sitting here with a man who is disguising himself because of pickles. It's nighttime, and he's wearing sunglasses indoors.

As if reading my mind Peter lowers his sunglasses and glances at the menu. I guess the coast is clear and there aren't any pickle spies dining tonight.

Now that I'm looking closely at Peter, I can see the resemblance to Carter. His eyes, his shoulders, the shape of his lips. He's like a shorter version of Carter with lighter hair.

Maybe Mrs. Parton is blond and not a fake one like Cousin Dolly.

I am sure they are not related, but my mind just can't stop going there.

Is that why I was attracted to Peter the other night – not because of Dolly Parton, although she's lovely, but because he looks like Carter – and he paid attention to me when Carter brought me to his family's weird funeral party and largely ignored me.

We order our burgers and Peter tells me that they are cremating Uncle Bernard on Friday, and his ashes will be spread at the basketball stadium on Saturday.

While I am now beyond starving, I'm glad I don't have any food in my mouth yet.

"Wait, what? They are sprinkling his ashes at a basketball game. You mean at home, right?" There could easily be a whole sports complex on the property that I've missed.

"No, the family has a box at the university's stadium – it's March Madness. Don't you know that?"

Oh, it's fucking March madness all right.

"So, you mean they are going to bring his ashes and sprinkle them...?"

"Outside in the garden, of course. What, did you think they were going to drop them on the court? You're so funny, Addison."

Yeah, that's me, a regular comedian. Everything has been so normal so far this week – why would I think the Lemieux family would do something off the wall?

The server brings our plates and I notice that Peter isn't eating any pickles. Now I guess he has pickle guilt because I would assume he *likes* pickles. They were probably his first solid food.

I grab the ketchup and load up my plate for lots of French fry dipping. Not a testicle in sight on my plate tonight.

I never would have thought I'd count that as a win until I came to Kentucky.

"So, what's on tomorrow's agenda? No one has given me the schedule for the week and every day is a big surprise."

I feel like I should ask because you just never know with these people.

Peter is chewing a big bite of burger and reaches for his napkin to wipe the mustard off his face. I can't believe how hungry we are after every meal at the Lemieux's place. Well, today more food was thrown than eaten.

"Carter is doing a terrible hosting job with you. I don't understand why he brought you here. Well, I kind of do, but anyway... tomorrow is horseback riding."

Of course it is.

"Do you ride?" He takes a gulp of his beer and looks eager to hear all about my equestrian accomplishments.

Carter warned me – bourbon, horses, and basketball. Three things I have zero interest in and even less experience with, but some impulsive part of my brain just wanted to put space between me and Declan.

"Haha... um... no... fun fact... I am allergic to horses."

"Wow, so you really didn't review the brochure before you booked this fun vacation."

He seems to notice my distress and adds, "I'm kidding. I know you left Annapolis to get away from a bad situation, and no one here is judging you. And if they dared to, you surely could get enough dirt on any of them to make them shut up."

He laughs and shakes his head.

Is he referring to the dirt that caused his fudged birth certificate or some other... I don't even want to know.

"I'm not here to butt into anyone's business, and Carter did warn me about the family's interests."

"It's not just the family – it's really Bernard's interests. He was the one who loved all of the many things we are experiencing this week." He laughs and says, "Kind of makes me hope I'm not hanging around this family anymore when Caroline goes, right?"

Actually, I think Caroline's interests are much better, but I don't even want to think about her right now because I am trying very hard not to think about what she told me.

I just smile and stuff more food in my mouth. Peter takes this as an invitation to keep talking, which is fine with me. The less I talk, the more likely I am to make it through this meal without something bad slipping out of my mouth.

As it is, Peter thinks my lack of interest in a deceased man's hobbies is the biggest thing on my mind.

"You know who loves the horses? Carter. He is wild for them. He'll be showing off his skills tomorrow for sure. But stick with me and you won't be bored."

He smiles, and was that a little eyebrow wiggle? No, that's ridiculous. No one under the age of seventy flirts with their eyebrows.

Still, Peter is pleasant company, and I don't feel as uncomfortable around him as I do Carter.

"Peter, I hope you don't mind me asking, but what did you mean when you said you know why Carter brought me here?"

He folds his napkin and leans forward with a lowered voice. "That's simple. Carter has never had an easy time with women. I think it all goes back to his weird relationship with my sister. Or should I say non-relationship? I think he broke her heart in high school, but it's never stopped her from pursuing him, even after she met Tyler and tricked him into marrying her."

"But what does that have to do with me?"

"He likes to bring dates to family events to keep Laura at a distance. But it never works, and she just ends up either trying even harder to get his attention, or she does something to sabotage his relationship with the new woman."

He studies my face, which I know is breaking out in a non-poker face look of alarm, and says, "But don't worry, she's soooo pregnant and I don't think she has the energy to pull any shenanigans. Plus, you're with me now and she wouldn't dare."

Hmm... I may be *with him* right at this moment, but does he think I'm *with him* with him? We are just eating a damn burger.

I just smile and accept a somewhat sticky dessert menu from the happy server, who has returned at the perfect moment. A nice brownie sundae might divert my attention from my overzealous dining partner and the impending horse contact that is sure to come tomorrow.

Whether I have a future with Carter, Peter, or the cute little dog in my earlier fantasy, I know one thing for sure.

Uncle Bernard and I would not have been compatible.

Episode 21
They're Not Baseball Players

The house is blissfully quiet at this hour, after the earlier mania.

Peter dropped me off and fortunately did not try to kiss me goodnight. I've always been pretty good at giving guys the "no" vibes without having to say the word, but I will gladly say it if I need to.

It's not that I don't want to kiss Peter – I just want to make better decisions with my life, and especially my love life, going forward.

Now that I've had some time to reflect on my choices, I started dating Declan in my freshman year of college because *he liked me*, and I didn't take the time to evaluate how much I liked him.

Someday I will go for therapy to find out why my self-esteem is so low. Maybe Scarlet can help me.

Wait... never mind... it's her brothers I am caught between.

Brothers... yeah, she is the one who will need therapy when she finds out the truth about her family.

I was grateful the door was unlocked as I tiptoed into the foyer a moment ago. I didn't even think about the fact that I don't have a key.

I would think they would lock their doors... unless someone is waiting up for me.

Luckily, I don't have to go into the living room or the parlor or whatever they call it in order to go to my room... or any room I might decide to visit.

My shoes are making too much noise on the floor, so I bend over to take them off and almost fall over when I hear, "Did you have a nice night?"

Thank God that's a woman's voice. Not that I think Bernard would be talking to me, but if this place were haunted that would be the last straw.

Camille waves from one of the stuffy sofas in the living room and beckons me to join her. It's almost pitch dark, but I can see her silhouette in the moonlight streaming through the floor-to-ceiling window.

I cringe and hope she can't see my facial expression. These people have been so hospitable to me, with no interference at all as to why I'm even here or the nature of my relationship with their son.

I put my shoes back on and walk toward the chair next to her, where she has now turned on a dim light.

"Hi, Mrs. Lemieux. I did have a nice night, thank you. I guess you're having a little 'you' time after the earlier festivities."

I glance around the room and notice that something is missing.

"Call me Cammy. And Addison, Bernard isn't here anymore. Well, he isn't anywhere since he's dead, but the body has been removed. You didn't think we were going to keep his body on display in the house all week, did you?"

She raises an eyebrow and I smile and say, "No, of course not, but it's your house so..."

"Sit down, and let's chat. Would you like some tea?"

She gestures to the beautiful teapot sitting on the coffee table in the shape of a horse. The teapot, not the coffee table. A horse would make a poor surface for serving food and drink.

"No thank you, I was just going up to bed. It sounds like you have another big day planned tomorrow."

"Oh yes, we are having quite the week. I'm glad we don't have a bigger family because these weeklong celebrations get to be a little much."

She sips her tea and daintily places the cup back in the saucer. "I know we do things rather unconventionally here, and you've been such a good sport about it."

I wave my hand and say, "I'm a stranger and you've welcomed me into your home with very few questions asked. Of course, whatever you do is fine – everyone has been so nice."

I'm not sure where this conversation is going and I don't feel prepared to answer questions, but why would Camille ask me to sit with her? I'm sure she's had her fill of people for the day.

Also, I have questions I wish I could ask her, but Carter is the only person I have any right to talk to in this house about anything Caroline told me.

And that's only if I have intentions of pursuing him. Or being pursued.

I don't think I will be prepared for Caroline's full moon intention ceremony by tomorrow. Maybe by 2025? I'm sure there will be more moons of all sizes then, too.

"Addison, I spoke with Caroline earlier. She told me, after much cajoling... she was crying in her room so loudly I had to intervene... that she shared some personal family information with you today. She was very upset because she felt like she'd betrayed my and Claude's trust. But really, it's about time we deal with this."

I'm glad it's still rather dark in here because my face feels as red as my hair.

"Oh, Mrs... Cammy... she did tell me something but don't worry, I won't tell anyone. It's none of my business."

"I disagree. It is your business if you have any interest in my son. I see the way Carter looks at you and I don't want my lifestyle to scare off the first nice girl he's ever brought home."

Her lifestyle? More like her husband's. It's so typical of a woman to blame herself for a man's actions.

"I haven't noticed him looking at me any way, honestly, and I don't understand why he brought me here. Although, before we arrived at the house, he was much happier and a little flirty. I don't really understand what's going on."

Camille leans back onto the soft nest of silk brocade throw pillows and says, "Carter is always on edge when the Partons are around, especially Laura. I told Carter that Peter and Laura were his half-siblings after he confessed that he'd kissed Laura at the junior prom. I felt like I had no choice but to be honest with him. Laura didn't know and she had been trying to push their relationship beyond friendship ever since they'd hit puberty."

"So, Carter wasn't interested?"

She sighs and says, "I think on some level he sensed something wasn't right. Maybe he has a little of his cousin Caroline's intuition. I don't know, but I felt I had to take charge of the situation. Neither my husband nor the Partons had taken any steps to tell the kids the truth."

I purse my lips and struggle to tread lightly with my

next question, but I am determined to get more information now that I'm in this deep.

"If you don't mind me asking, why are the Partons always around? It seems to me you would not want constant reminders of your husband's infidelity in your life. And Peter said that you and your husband are best friends with his parents. I don't get it."

She rubs her temples and says, "I do wish this had all come to a head a different week, but maybe bringing the family together for Bernard's send-off is the best opportunity to come clean, after all these years."

Okay, this is where she's going to admit to a crime or a cover-up.

Wait, maybe they're spies, like Erica's boyfriend, who is *allegedly* an accountant. They all pretend to be something else... no, that makes no sense.

I got it! Mr. Parton is sterile, and Claude is the friendly neighborhood sperm donor.

"Addison, this may be shocking to you, but Claude and I have been in a relationship with Franklin and Eloise Parton since our honeymoons."

This just keeps getting weirder.

"Yes, I know you've been friends for a long time. How is that shocking? I can see that it would be hard to ruin the friendship without telling the truth..."

She's shaking her head.

"No, we have been in a *relationship* with them. It started out as a little wild hot tub fun when we met them on our honeymoon in Jamaica and then... we all fell in love."

The realization of what she is telling me hits my brain like a sack of rocks and I am suddenly looking for an exit.

Not just from the room... the house... the state...

What the hell should I say to that?

I have to say something because she's staring at me.

"So, you're saying that you all... *all* of you... with *all* of you?"

"Yes, that's what I'm saying. I know it's very odd and unacceptable to most people, but it has worked for us for more than thirty years and it keeps our marriages strong. Unfortunately, we realized that Franklin was sterile and that Claude was the one getting both of us pregnant. And in the case of the first two kids, at the same time."

I blink my eyes rapidly and say, "And no one knows this but Caroline?"

"She walked in on something once and we swore her to secrecy. It was a long time ago and Claude's parents were still alive. They were very religious, and they would have been destroyed. They probably would have disinherited him. So, yes, we offered Caroline a lot of perks for her silence, and I realize now what an unfair and terrible burden we placed on her for our own selfishness."

She pauses and adds, "You must think we're monsters."

I clear my throat and say, "No, I don't know what to think, honestly. It's a lot to process. Does Carter know...everything?"

"He does. I had to tell him because as you can imagine his first inclination was that his father was cheating and that just wasn't true at all."

"Thank you for telling me this. I truly didn't deserve this information. But it does help me to understand Carter's behavior since we've been here. I was going to go see him. Now. Do you think I should?"

She refills her tea and says, "It depends. Is there anything between you and Peter?"

"No, not really. He's a nice guy, but he..."

"Just reminds you of Carter, and gave you the attention Carter was withholding? I get that. I would just ask, as a mother, that you don't pursue Carter unless you are sure Peter is out of the picture. When we tell them all the truth, it's going to be a huge strain on their already difficult relationships, and the boys don't need to be vying for the same woman's affections."

I nod my head. "Understood. And Camille, I am not ready to jump into anything new right now. I just want to talk to your son. Be with him. Offer him... something... I'm not sure what yet. Does that make sense?"

"Yes, it does." She stands up and opens her arms and I step into her embrace. I am not a huge hugger, but it isn't every day your possible future mother-in-law tells you she's a swinger, and there isn't a baseball bat in sight.

I was not taught the etiquette for this situation. The only swinging my parents do is on the front porch.

Episode 22
Room Service

I swear this house is bigger than the Inn I used to mismanage; I mean manage.

Damn Declan, getting in my head, making me think I wasn't doing a good job. He better stay at said Inn because I have no time or energy to deal with him now that I've added swingers to the list of things weirding me out... I thought sheep's testicles, a dead body in the living room, and an old lady calling me "the fuck it girl" was already enough.

Where the hell is Carter's room? I can't believe I still can't find it, although I've been putting all my concentration into finding my own room.

Crap, this is the hall with all the horse names. Is he in the Palomino room or the Clydesdale?

I think this is the one – I remember it being on a corner just before the staircase that leads to my wing.

Now that I'm here I realize I should have texted first. It's not 1975 when people have to go knocking on doors. The "surprise guest" has gone the way of the pay phone.

Well, I'm here now so I might as well knock. I hope I won't be disturbing anyone sleeping in the other nearby rooms, although it's not an actual hotel. I don't think too many family members are staying here.

I knock lightly and I hear movement in the room. Hopefully, I didn't wake him up.

Oh, now I hear voices. Maybe he's not alone – this

will be very awkward if he has a woman in there.

He could just be watching TV... okay the door is opening... oh no...

"Oh, I'm so sorry... Mr... Sir..."

For a moment I can't remember which side of the family Uncle Gaston belongs to.

"Mr. Dumas, that's right. You're Camille's brother. You work in the mortuary business with the bodies... I mean with Camille... not the actual bodies... she's the doctor. Anyway, I am so sorry to disturb you. I was... um... trying to find Carter's room."

So not only am I rambling about surprising a man in his bedroom, I am also trying not to insinuate that Gaston shouldn't be working with the bodies because of... well you know... I had almost forgotten about that because of the other new thing...

Too many things...

Uncle Gaston is quite handsome for an older man, and I can't help but notice that he must have been quite the popular guy in his day. Never mind... he's rich and hot but I would bet morticians have dating issues.

"It's quite all right, Miss. Carter's room is on the other side of this floor. It's like a mirror so very easy to get lost."

From inside the room, I hear, "Gaston, we're not finished."

My ears do a double take and I try to hide my reaction.

Was that Eleanor from the shop? The same Eleanor who was walking up to the main house with Austin a few hours ago?

She likes them young and old? In the same night?

Who *are* these people?

"I am coming!" He shakes his head and whispers, "This girl, her prices are good, but she always wants to provide more value. It's crazy, but I guess I should be happy. Have a good night with my nephew."

He winks and closes the door.

Her *prices*?

Please let her be selling something. Like a product. Amway... Avon... a nice Pampered Chef frying pan.

Well, it's none of my business – I say that a lot lately – so I saunter off to find Carter.

Hopefully Eleanor, or whoever is in there didn't give the family a three-for-one deal tonight.

Carter is standing in his doorway when I round the corner, looking adorable and hot at the same time in his jogger sweatpants and soft blue henley sleep shirt.

His hair is sticking up all over the place as if he has been thinking hard and rubbing his head is how he jump-starts his brain.

I stop abruptly and say, "Hey."

"Hey, I heard you and I wondered why you were over on the other hall. What's up?"

I am not going to tell him about Gaston because... wait for it... it's none of my business.

I should get a t-shirt made with that saying and Lexington, Kentucky embroidered on it as a souvenir of this trip.

"Can I come in?"

He jumps out of the way and motions for me to enter. "I'm sorry, of course. Why didn't you text? I would have come down to get you. Unless you didn't want Peter to see me. Or me to see Peter."

"There is no Peter. I mean there is a guy named Peter, but he went home. I was talking to your mother.

And Caroline earlier..."

He sits on the edge of his bed, leaving me standing awkwardly still wearing my ugly black sweatshirt from the corn dog throwing party.

"You were talking to them about Peter?"

"No, why would I... fair enough. But he just bought me a burger. It's not like I -"

"... had sex in the driveway with him?"

"What? Of course not! How much drama do you think I need in what... three days?"

"Okay, sorry. What were you talking to them about?"

I pull up the upholstered chair that matches the fancy writing desk and sit down in front of Carter.

"They told me some things about you... and the family. Caroline told me about the sibling thing... and then your mother told me... the other thing."

His hair starts taking a beating again as he vigorously rubs his head and rolls his shoulders.

"This family is so fucking exhausting. I should have taken you somewhere else."

"But I wouldn't have gone anywhere else. Remember, the deal clincher was talking to your mother, who seemed like a nice lady. I mean, she still is a nice lady... there is just more than meets the eye."

"Yeah, it's not been easy. So, I guess you understand at least some of what's going on with Laura, then? But not the part about how she's married and about to have her fourth child but still hasn't given up on me. No one understands that part."

I look around the room stalling for time before I phrase the next bombshell.

Wringing my hands the same way Carter works on

his hairdo, I blurt out, "Your mother plans on making all of this known to the whole family... and Laura and Peter... I think before the end of the week."

I bite my lip and eye the door – I may need to run because there is such a thing as kill the messenger.

Maybe not *kill*, but at least seriously *freak out* on the messenger.

Carter starts laughing and throws himself back on the bed.

Okay, now he's lost it. Should I call someone? Leave? Give him a pill? Does he have pills?

I stand over him and say, "Are you okay?"

He smiles up at me and gently pulls me down beside him. I sit on the cozy comforter, and he reaches up with one hand and pulls me down, gently kissing me on the forehead, the nose, and the lips.

It's a soft kiss – the kind where you know there's passion behind it but there's something else much deeper stirring... or maybe he's so happy with this news he wants to kiss the messenger instead of kill.

I don't have a lot of experience with men.

And zero experience with men whose parents are swingers and have secret half-siblings.

All new to me.

And to think I thought the week-long funeral was the odd thing about this family.

Episode 23
The Stable is Unstable

"Come on, just come meet the horses. They're really beautiful, gentle animals. Look, I even have gloves for you to wear."

Carter is desperately trying to lure me into the smelly place where the big, itch-inducing beasts live, but I am afraid I am going to come out looking like one big hive.

Although, I tested positive for horse allergy when I was a child and I've never tested it in real life. It could be no big deal, and if I appease Carter, he will be happy and go about his horsey business and this part of the funeral festivities will be over.

I wanted to get back to talking to Scarlet. I hadn't connected with her since our shopping trip, and I could use some girl time with a woman my own age.

As soon as Carter and I arrived together, she cornered me and asked me what was going on. Apparently, the whole family knows I spent the night in his room. Either the rooms are bugged, or Gaston doesn't respect my privacy as much as I respect his.

I told her that I did spend the night but all we did was sleep after a few kisses. He respects my boundaries and my need to take it slow after ending a ten-year relationship.

Also, I don't think that talking about his parents' unconventional sex life was much of a turn-on for him.

It was nice to just talk and fall asleep together.

Scarlet kept grabbing my arm and smiling as if she already sees our wedding in the family's future.

Oh my God, what do they do for weddings if they do all of this for a funeral?

I don't even want to think about it.

She hugged me and said, "This is so exciting. Now maybe you'll want to stick around longer. I know… you could take over running the Inn. I am so over it."

She looked at me with the wonder of a little kid getting ready to throw a corn dog at a funeral cookout, but I had to burst her bubble.

I am not going backwards, and I now have a no-family business policy for my employment future. That would be like going from the frying pan into a pit of flaming spiders.

Plus, do I really want to work in hospitality anymore? In just a few days away from Annapolis, Declan, and The O'Shaughnessy, I feel different.

She understood and I fell a little bit in sisterhood love with her for that.

Not that Erica wouldn't support my decisions, but Scarlet is a little more touchy-feely than my tough sibling.

I'm still standing in front of the horse stable and now I see Peter has shown up and is helping himself to some breakfast and coffee from the refreshments table – also, where do these things come from? It's like magic – I never see anyone setting anything up and it's all just there.

It's probably Caroline. I think she's the most underappreciated family member and I hope all this drama with the swinging and the surprise siblings doesn't make her life even harder.

"Okay, I'll go meet a horse or two."

Carter brightens as I give in to his request. It is a simple thing to make someone happy, and besides I would like to avoid Peter until I decide how to want to "be" with him after our "sort of" date.

Carter pulls me close and gives me a sneaky kiss because no one's looking and puts the gloves on my hands.

I'm sure no one saw us, although Grandma Dominique and Camille are hanging out close to the stables, and Camille is telling her mother that it's too early to put bourbon in her coffee.

The family matriarch is like ninety years old, so she either just started drinking since she decided to embrace the "fuck it" lifestyle, or she's an old pro.

"This is my favorite horse. Her name is Dusty. Come here, she wants you to pet her."

I'm pretty sure Dusty just wants food and for all these people to leave her alone. I know people develop relationships with their horses, but don't they get spooked easily, especially when there are a lot of people around?

At least it's a weekday and all the family's children are in school. I'm pretty sure if you super-soaked a horse, it would break down this little wooden door and that would be... not good at all.

I brace myself to touch Dusty's neck. I do have to admit that her greyish fur is clean and sleek and she's very calm. Oh okay, that's not so bad. She seems to like it.

Carter nods approvingly and says, "See, she likes you. It's too bad you can't feel how silky her coat is. Why don't you just take off a glove and try it? If you get itchy, there's a sink over there and you could wash your hands right away. And I know my mom has every medical remedy in the house. I'm sure Benadryl cream would do the trick."

Hmm... I don't know... he's probably right. I'm being silly. I also tested positive for cats and dogs, and I've spent time at friends' homes with pets and I've been fine.

"Okay, I'll try it."

I take off the glove slowly and then begin to pet Dusty. She seems happier, as if she knew that was a fake hand, so to speak. She's warm and soft, and aww... now she's nuzzling my...

"Hey, there's some asshole out here looking for you, Addison."

Austin is standing in the doorway holding an enormous coffee cup and sporting crazier bed hair than Carter had last night. But I don't think Austin's is from worrying, just sleeping. He is still blissfully unaware that there is anything more worrisome in life than getting up early for another funeral event.

Carter shakes his head and says, "Come on, that's not a nice way to talk about Peter. He's our b... buddy."

Austin rolls his eyes. "I'm not talking about the pickle prince... he heard about where Addison slept last night and threw his coffee on the ground and ran off. Such a little baby gherkin."

My chest tightens as I say, "Who is here then? Shit, does he have blond hair, piercing blue eyes, and an overabundance of anger?"

Austin points at me and says, "Bingo, that's the guy. Uh oh, I hear him tussling with Mom and Grandma now, and she's deep into the bourbon coffee." He mimics her drinking and swaying. "She's even got the cane today – this could become a good show. I think I'll get my video rolling just in case it's TikTok-worthy when she whacks him."

Carter makes his way to the entrance and moves his brother to this side.

"Nobody is whacking anybody." He stands in the doorway and says, "Declan, you need to get off my property. Addison doesn't want to see you."

Hmm... I don't know if that's *entirely* true, but I don't want to see him like this. And I did tell Carter last night that I hope he doesn't show up... so I can see why he's trying to be all valiant and get rid of him.

Okay, Carter doesn't really know Declan and he isn't going to back down. I hope he didn't bring his cousins. The police at a funeral event would be unfortunate. I need to stop petting Dusty and intervene.

Crap... I was just petting Dusty for a long time. Now my eye is itchy. Did I touch my eye?

Declan comes bounding into the stable and already the horses are getting restless. I don't think Declan has ever seen a horse up close so he is blissfully unaware that they could mow him down like a herd of Black Friday shoppers at Walmart.

Except there are no cheap TVs here... only horse poop.

"Addison, I have come to take you home. I can't believe you willingly left town with a stranger." He pokes Carter in the chest and says, "I should report you for human trafficking."

"Declan, stop it. I did come willingly and what the hell are you doing here? How did you find me?"

He's lucky that Carter was raised to be a gentleman

with self-control, because if the shoe were on the other foot, or should I say – the poking was on the other chest, Declan would have Carter in a headlock by now.

Declan is pacing and every time he passes a horse they whine and a few of them have started jumping up in the air on their back feet. As much as I want him to leave, I don't want a horse stampede to be his escort home.

Or to the hospital.

Or God forbid, the basement of this house.

Uncle Bernard doesn't need any company and death isn't a suitable punishment for being a hot-headed dumbass.

Declan punches the palm of his hand. "Seriously? You run off with the bourbon guy and you think I can't track you down. These rich fuckers are famous, especially here in this shit-kicking town."

Okay, now I think a few horses have made fresh poops by the smell of it. They're either protesting the insults of their homeland or they are getting the anxiety poops.

"Declan, let's go out front and talk about this calmly. This family has done nothing wrong. They've been very hospitable."

"Oh, I bet they have. Just like my family has been for the last ten years!"

"You *fired* me! Don't tell me that wasn't your parents' decision?"

"I asked you to *marry* me – why are you fixated on the stupid job? And how can you work hotel hours and have six kids?"

Austin, who has been enjoying the show, says, "Wow, Addison, you have a lot in common with the brood mares in here."

Declan says, "Who the fuck are you and are you calling my fiancée a horse?"

Carter steps forward again and says, "She is not your fiancée. Now I want you off my property."

Austin is still taking random clips of video and honestly, I'm glad because we may need it for evidence of an impending crime.

"I'm pretty sure this isn't *your* property and it's owned by those big-assed old ladies out there. Shit, Addison of course this guy thinks you're hot, have you seen the asses on the women in this family? There's a chick out there your age who could carry a full place setting on her-"

"That does it!"

Oh great, now Dominique is running into the stable, with her cane in one hand and her boozy coffee sloshing in the other.

Camille is behind her. "Mother, stop it. You're going to hurt yourself."

This stable was not made for this many people and now the horses are in full freak-out mode, and I swear the walls are shaking.

Just as Camille tries to reach for her mother to steady her, Dominique loses her footing, recovers, and whacks Declan in the back of the knees with her cane.

Down he goes like a fresh horse poo and before anyone can help him up, Dominique is pouring her coffee on his head. Jeez... I hope that's not hot... holy crap, Dusty just broke down her door and Declan takes the full brunt of it as he was trying to scramble to his knees.

"Declan, are you okay?"

My voice is drowned out by the multiple people yelling as more horses begin escaping and wow, my fingers are itchy. I look down for one second at my reddening hand and take a hoof to the ankle and uh oh... night, night...

Episode 24
Forced Proximity

Maybe if I just keep my eyes shut and pretend to be asleep, I won't have to hear all about the aftermath of Declan's uninvited appearance at horse day.

I did get the wind knocked out of me and Camille also thinks I fainted, but I don't have a concussion, so I was allowed to take to my bed alone like a Civil War era debutante with a too-tight corset.

I'm in my bed... well, my bed for as long as they let me stay here now that I've caused a major incident.

I can only hope all the horses were rounded up and that they were able to get someone to fix all the stall doors in the stable. As I was led away from the scene of the crime, the stable was at least standing, so that's something.

Declan was totally out of line and being a complete asshole, but I'm sorry – someone needs to confiscate that old lady's alcohol and weapons.

Or at least not allow her to be in possession of both at the same time.

I hope Declan is okay, but if he has lived to tell about this incident he will rewrite the history. I smile as I think of him telling his cousins that he was taken out by a ninety-year-old lady with a big butt and a horse door.

A voice breaks my thoughts as I chastise myself for joking about Declan living through the incident. He is a jerk, but I don't want him to die.

"Hey, why are you smiling? Did my mother give you the good drugs?"

I open my eyes to find Carter on the edge of my bed, and the daylight waning outside my window.

I sit up a little and then sink back down into my pillows. I think it is time for more drugs. I may not have a concussion, but I have the mother of all regular headaches.

"She probably did but they're worn off now. But I guess I don't deserve them anyway."

Carter takes my hand and says, "Why would you say that?"

"Oh, come on, Declan wouldn't have been here causing trouble if it wasn't for me. Although your grandmother certainly escalated the situation."

"Yeah, I think she could use an intervention. Bernard's death has her thinking that she's next and she's kind of off the rails. But that's still no excuse to attack someone, and obviously, between Austin and I, we could have physically subdued him if needed."

I wince and sigh. "Where is my overzealous former boyfriend? He really got walloped – those horses are powerful animals."

"He's downstairs with my mother."

My stomach does a flip, and my eyes widen. "He's in the living room having tea, right? Not in the morgue room? Come on, he's not dead, is he? You have that 'someone's dead' look on your face."

He holds up his hands and says, "Jeez, no, he's not dead. Also, we don't call it 'the morgue room.' But he did take a beating and he does have a concussion. My mother is going to come up and talk to you more about it in a minute, but I just wanted to see you and make sure you're okay. Honestly, I partially blame myself for this because we knew Declan was plotting a visit and it was stupid for us to think he was going to give up or not be able to find you."

"It wasn't your responsibility. I just wish he could leave. What's going to happen now? Are your parents pressing charges?"

"Knock, knock, no we're not."

Camille glides into the room carrying a tray of water, dinner, and pills. She looks perfectly put together, which is amazing after the ordeal of this day.

"Now, Addison, take two of these, drink plenty of water, and see if you can eat something. I think by tomorrow you'll be feeling better."

I sit up and pop the pills in my mouth and swallow them with a big gulp of water.

"Thanks so much, and I can't apologize enough for... all of it. I understand if you'd like me to leave after I'm well enough to travel. Or maybe you want me to stay until I can leave with Declan."

Carter kisses me on the top of the head and says, "This is my cue to go. I'm going to swing by the stables and see how the repair crew is doing, and I'll see you tomorrow. Get some rest."

He walks out and I sigh deeply. Why tomorrow? Why not tonight? If there was ever a time for a cuddle fest in Carter's room, it's tonight.

And who knows, maybe it could turn into something more.

But maybe he doesn't want that now that he sees all the baggage I still have, and probably will continue to have for some time. I doubt Declan has seen the light and the error of his ways just because of a good whack to the head, and so far, I have been terrible at setting boundaries.

Camille watches Carter walk out the door and turns back to me. "I know what you're thinking, but he's just giving you some space. Now let's talk about that ex of yours."

"Okay, what are we going to do with him?" I smile to lighten the mood, but I seriously don't know the answer, and I am hoping Camille will take care of it. It makes my head hurt even more knowing he's still under this roof.

He could be walking around causing new problems right now. It's not like they have him locked in a dungeon in chains.

Although I've never been to the often-mentioned but never visited "downstairs," it does have an ominous tone if you think about what's down there.

Uncle Bernard is down there – I just know it.

Camille looks at the ceiling and purses her lips. "Well, for starters he got a good talking to once he woke up and I knew he was out of the woods. I told him that we would not press charges – my mother *did* attack him with her cane, which was the tipping point for the horses, so to speak. Fortunately, no one else was hurt and the horses all seem to be fine as well."

"But he was wrong to come to our property and behave the way he did. He is going to be okay, but he suffered a concussion. I've been sitting with him but frankly, I have a lot to do for tomorrow's planned activities, so you are going to spend the night with him and make sure he's okay."

"What? I can't do that. That's exactly what he wants, and how will I know if he's okay?"

I lower my voice because really he is my problem and continue. "I'm sorry, I know I am responsible, but does he really need someone to watch him?"

"It would be for the best. And Addison, you need to talk to Declan. I mean really talk to him. You just broke up after a proposal and a ten-year relationship and ran off with the bourbon guy to a funeral. Now, I think you seem perfectly stable, but when we examine the facts... I just want you to make a good decision before you move forward. It's bad enough I have my own bombshell to drop on the family... my son doesn't need his heart broken. And sending Declan off in anger isn't going to solve anything."

I am suddenly no longer hungry even though that soup smelled good a minute ago.

"You're right. I'll talk to him. I owe him that much, and all of you, especially Carter."

She tilts her head and says, "Well, you really owe it to yourself more than anyone. I have a feeling that if you start making decisions a bit more selfishly, you'll make better ones."

She watches me for my response, but I just nod in agreement.

She's good at this mom thing. My mom is, too, and they would like each other. But I can't imagine a world where my mom and Camille would ever meet. Too much has happened already to spoil things with Carter before they have begun.

Camille hops up and says, "Now, that's settled. Declan will be escorted here shortly."

"Here? In this room? There's only one bed."

"Didn't you sleep together at home?"

"Well yes, sometimes but we are supposed to be

broken up."

Camille folds her arms across her chest and says, "Young lady, you need to be sure you are over this man, and there is no better way than to share a bed, your matching head injuries, and a good talk."

I can see this is happening and sure, I could refuse, but Camille is right about this, too. I left Annapolis in anger, and I need to see if I feel the same about the breakup now that the anger has subsided.

"Okay, send him up, and thanks for everything."

I pick up my spoon and ask for the information no one ever provides, even though I now know the family's deepest secrets.

"What's on the agenda for tomorrow's funeral activities?"

Camille rolls her eyes and says, "Bourbon tasting and a Muppet movie marathon. I keep saying those things don't go together but maybe the presence of the kids will keep the adults from overindulging. Bernard was a huge Muppets fan. Well, I'll be off. And Addison, if you need Declan to be removed from the room just call and I'll send someone up. You need to talk but he also needs to behave."

Do they have bouncers I haven't seen?

And *The Muppets*, really? Peter and I joked about that, but Bernard actually did like his pigs and frogs on the big screen as well as on his plate.

Oh... Peter... there's another person I should talk to, although will he care about his love life when he finds out his father isn't his father?

I mean, the poor guy was worried about cheating with the wrong pickles. He doesn't exactly have a tough skin when it comes to his family.

Episode 25
Pillow Talk

"This may be the weirdest experience of my life."

Declan is comfortably lounging in my king-sized bed in the lavender room, which is really messing with the overall feng shui and whatever else is supposed to be beneficial to my mental health in this room.

Unfortunately, I am in the same bed, and we look like nineteenth-century twins who've been tucked into bed by the nanny for an extended recovery from one of the non-fatal plagues.

I look over at my long-term, now ex-boyfriend and say, "It's not super normal for me either."

Declan rubs his forehead and says, "This place is bigger than our... my... The O'Shaughnessy... they could have put me in a different room. Or I could have just left. I'm not saying I don't appreciate it after... everything... but I want you to know that I did not ask for this."

He motions at our bizarre situation, and I nod.

"I believe you. Camille is a wonderful woman, but she's eccentric. In more ways than one, but let's not go there."

There is no way I am letting Declan know what's about to go down with this family because it makes his crew look like *The Brady Bunch*.

"All I know is that my head is pounding, and I regret coming here. I can see you're done with me."

He is not going to make me feel sorry for him, but I

need to control my anger.

I sigh and say, "I shouldn't have left so dramatically but the opportunity presented itself and I don't know... I guess I just wanted to do something crazy and spontaneous for once."

Declan smirks and says, "Yeah, you are kind of boring."

I smack him and remember that he has multiple injuries.

"Ow... jeez... okay, too soon for jokes." He rubs his shoulder.

"But seriously I get it. Our whole relationship has been pretty mundane and it's good we're getting out while we're young."

And together we sing, "Because tramps like us, baby we were born to run!"

The other thing I forgot to mention is that Declan's family is obsessed with Bruce Springsteen.

See, every family has quirks, not just the Dumas-Lemieux clan.

Maybe I do have a head injury if I am comparing weeklong themed funerals and four people in a marriage to loving the greatest rock icon of all time.

Okay, maybe I was a tad bit brainwashed.

Declan shifts in an effort to get more comfortable and says, "Yeah, the Boss is always there for us. See, that's what this crazy funeral week needs – a Bruce night." He shakes his head and says, "So, these people seriously have a funeral for a whole week every time someone dies?"

"I thought it was weird at first, too, but they aren't like your family where the parents have forty-seven first cousins and someone dies once a quarter at least. They make it a family reunion. And sure, some of the family members have some issues, but who doesn't?"

"So, is it the family you like or the guy?"

I continue to stare at the ceiling because it's always been my preferred way of having awkward conversations with Declan. I suppose that should have also been a sign that we weren't a match made in heaven. You should be able to look the love of your life in the eye.

"I do like Carter, but things have been weird... to say the least." I motion back and forth between us to signify the culmination of the week's weirdness and how in the hell is it only Tuesday night?

"Yeah, he's probably an okay guy, especially if he brought you here and he hasn't tried anything. Just be careful, Addison, alright? Maybe you should go visit your folks in Michigan for a while. Take some time to clear your head before jumping into anything. And don't worry about money, my dad deposited a big severance check into your account."

"Wow, thanks. I didn't even think about that. I would normally get all indignant and say I don't want anything from your family, but that's ridiculous. I earned it."

We sit in silence for a moment and just when I think he's fallen asleep, Declan takes my hand and whispers, "We had a good run."

My eyes get a little misty. "Yeah, we did." I squeeze his hand and add, "You should stick around this week. Who knows what other fun activities they have in store? Maybe there will be a drag queen leprechaun to remind you of home."

"I'd smack you with the pillow if I had any strength.

Now give me whatever drugs the scary French lady left on that nightstand."

I reach for the Tylenol, and I clink against a bottle of bourbon.

That's the last thing we need, although it is only Tuesday...

Episode 26
Everybody Loves Eleanor

My head doesn't feel too bad this morning and I was grateful to wake up alone.

Declan was also apparently feeling better and decided to leave. He texted me and told me he was on his way back to Annapolis.

So, imagine my surprise when I bumped into him on the way to the breakfast buffet (yes, this is just like a hotel).

Apparently, he had every intention of leaving, however, he ran into Camille on his way out and she marched him back downstairs to her "office" and checked him out before she would let him drive.

During the course of the examination, she suggested that he stay the rest of the week and join us in the other planned activities.

It was nice of her to treat Declan with respect and provide medical care after he showed up at her home acting like a maniac, but now I feel like she's just fucking with me.

Maybe she's just bored because the other half of her relationship has been away on a cruise, and her lawfully wedded husband, a death in the family, and a houseful of people aren't enough to keep her mentally stimulated.

And not to mention her decision to drop a major bombshell at the end of this glorious time together.

I told Declan I was fine with him staying if he

wanted to (why not just add to the insanity?), but he should probably find somewhere else to sleep. I do feel like we made our peace last night, but this is a bit fresh and new to sleep under the same roof as... well... everything that's going on under this roof.

Now we're eating breakfast together in the dining room as if no one else lives here. For some reason, this family seems to appear and disappear at all the right times.

He says, "No, I totally get that. I am going to stay at the family's little inn. The sister with the big... blue eyes... runs it and I was told they had a room for rent. It's nearby, but it gives us a little breathing room."

I butter my toast and say, "Okay, that's reasonable. But I really don't get why you want to stay here. You don't know anyone but me and we agreed to keep our distance for a while, and you didn't exactly endear yourself to the family. Although what these people find endearing is not exactly... typical."

He gulped his orange juice and wiped his mouth with the embroidered linen napkin. "I know, right? I'm just going with it. Things are nuts at home and I'm hoping if I lay low for a while my parents will sort out the mess at the Inn. And also... I hate to admit this, but you've already got your eye on a guy so... there is a woman here I'd like to spend some time with."

I mentally run through all the women and Scarlet is the only single young woman and Declan is clearly not interested in the butt circumference she's offering. Hmm... who else? Not Caroline?

I shouldn't say that. Caroline is very attractive but she's at least ten or more years older than Declan and I don't see him going for an older woman.

"Oh, well Scarlet has a boyfriend…"

"No, she's pretty and all, but you know I just can't… anyway, no it's not a member of this family."

He's only been here since yesterday afternoon and he has spent a good portion of that time yelling like a madman, getting knocked out by an old lady, and sleeping off the effects of the consequences of his actions.

Who has he met here who isn't related to the family? Laura wasn't even around, and she is obviously not available. And Declan wants his own big family, not someone else's.

"I give up." I shrug my shoulders and pick at my bacon. I am noticing that the breakfast food is so normal – either Bernard liked a traditional Grand Slam at Denny's or everyone is too tired to plan disgusting food themes for every meal.

"You've met Eleanor, right? She used to live in Annapolis."

Now my wheels are spinning faster than my relationship imploded.

Eleanor? He seriously knows Eleanor just because she lived in Annapolis for a short time and was dating a naval academy guy?

"Yes, I did meet her. She seems to be a friend of the family. How do you know her? She told me she was dating a guy at the naval academy."

He pushes his plate back and puts his hand on his stomach as he always does when he's full – as if he is signaling that he doesn't want any more food.

Never once have I tried to give him more food… or any food… so this must come from childhood force-feeding. Now that I think of it, his mother is always shoving more potatoes into people.

"Everyone knows Eleanor. She was dating that guy, but she was servicing half the town. She's very popular and good at what she does."

My eyes widen and I am trying to act naturally. Why is everyone acting like it's normal for Eleanor to be a prostitute? Am I supposed to call them sex workers now?

I mean, everyone has to make a living, but I do think it's illegal here and in Maryland... so why is everyone acting like this is so commonplace?

I get that the Dumas-Lemieux families are progressive, and not everyone knows how progressive.

But Declan comes from a strict Irish Catholic family, and I have never once heard him talk like this. Do you have to break up with someone to learn the truth about them?

Was she servicing Declan?

If I think about this too much, my bacon is going to resurface, and I would like to be well for the Muppet movie marathon tonight.

I can't believe that's my biggest goal right now – to watch movies that were made before I was born with one of the most bizarre groups of people I've ever met when those movies are readily available to watch on the Disney Channel at home.

Wherever home is now...

I clear my throat and say, "Yes, I'm sure she's very good. That's great. I'm sure she would like to... spend time with you, too."

"It's hard to know because she knew I was with you when she used to come to the Inn to service our guests."

Why did I think it was safe to take a drink?

"Hey, are you okay?"

Declan jumps up to pat my back as I choke on orange juice... and the fact that I was unknowingly running a brothel.

Episode 27
Crazy Mama

Peter slides over to the corner of the large movie-viewing room, where Carter and I are having a private moment after the insanity of the last day, well... several days.

I'm explaining why Declan is staying for his uncle's funeral celebrations (really his mother should explain as she's the loon who invited him) when Peter clears his throat and says, "So, Addison I guess the burgers weren't enough to win you over, huh?"

Carter rolls his eyes and I see his jaw start to tense up. I put my hand on his arm to calm him down and say to Peter, "I really hope you're not trying to start something because I think enough things have started. We are trying to settle things down."

Peter smiles and puts up his hands in mock exasperation.

"Me, start something? I would never. Seriously, I am only kidding. I heard you got roughed up when the mad Irishman stormed the horse barn. It sounds like an episode of Outlander but without the swords and nudity."

Carter sighs and says, "And yes, the mad Irishman is still here."

We all glance over at Declan and Eleanor, helping themselves to copious amounts of bourbon before the movies start. My guess is that they will bow out before the first film and go to wherever Eleanor is providing her services today.

I shoot Carter a look and he adds, "But it's not Addison's fault, my mother asked him to stay. She has an odd way of trying to bring people together."

She sure as hell does, and poor Peter is going to find out more of that in a few days, unless Carter can convince his parents to handle the situation differently.

Peter says, "Anyway, I'm glad to see you're okay. Your eyes were a mess when they first brought you out of the barn." He raises his glass and says, "I'm going to try a few more bourbons before *The Muppet Movie* starts. Haha...how often do you hear those words, am I right?"

He saunters off in the direction of Declan and Eleanor.

Maybe she has room for one more tonight.

I sigh and return my attention to Carter. I need to check my cattiness. Whatever Eleanor is doing, she seems a lot happier and more put together than me.

Carter leans back against the ornate chair rail, using it as a seat, and says, "You've really got all the men in a state this week."

He's smiling but I am getting tired of the teasing. "Hey, what did Peter mean about my eyes? I didn't injure my eyes in the fall."

Carter shifts his feet and says, "Oh yeah, about that. You were right about the horse thing. You are highly allergic. Your eyes swelled up like a puffer fish."

"What? Why didn't anyone tell me? How bad were they?"

"Well, there are photos."

"Photos?"

"My mother wanted to make sure we had

documentation in case something happened, and we had to rush you to a specialist."

He pulls out his phone and shows me a photo of a woman with red hair with two big swollen red, crusty balloons for eye sockets.

I let out a little yelp and silence myself so as not to draw attention to this horror.

"Oh my God, how did that happen?"

My mother said you must have touched your eye without realizing it but you should stay away from the horses. I'm sorry I caused that."

He pulls me in for a hug and I return it awkwardly as I feel many eyes in the room upon us.

"It's not your fault, you didn't know how bad it was."

"That's true, and tomorrow we're going to the cat sanctuary so you should be fine."

Just as I open my mouth to tell him that I'm also allergic to cats, a huge ruckus is walking into the room.

Well, the adults are walking, but their offspring are running and screaming. I wonder how illegal it would be to give them all just a little bit of bourbon.

Carter excuses himself to help his Aunt Violette get settled and Peter does the same for his sister and her husband. Laura allows Peter to deal with her kids while she tries to get Carter's attention.

Good luck with that as there is already one twin hanging off his leg imitating Animal from *The Muppets*.

I still don't understand how this is honoring the life of an old man. I strongly doubt Bernard spent much time with this crew or he wouldn't have lived so long.

I take this opportunity to sneak out of the room and walk across the hall to the empty library.

Whew... I could take a nap in here. I've seen the Muppet movies enough times to skip this activity. I should pretend I am allergic to children and go upstairs.

Just as I'm getting comfortable on one of the squishy sofas, I hear footsteps.

Maybe Carter wants to... oh boy... it's Hottie McHottiepants.

Jeremy (that's his actual name) is startled and says, "Oh sorry, I didn't think there was anyone in here. I just needed to... well... you know..."

"Calm your nerves for a minute?"

He flops onto the sofa across from me and says, "Oh my God, yes. Does that make me a bad husband and father?"

I sit up straighter and say, "Um... no... we all need a break sometimes and your kids are a bit of a handful."

He runs his hands through his thick dark hair, which only makes him look hotter.

"That's the understatement of the century. And I don't know why Violette insists on bringing them to these events. She can't drink and there is bourbon flowing all night, and our boys will fight with Laura's brats, and really it just helps me and Laura's husband to march to an earlier grave."

"Wow, that paints a picture. Yeah, it seems like... I don't know what to say... I don't have children."

He rubs his temples and says, "You know, I never thought I would either. And then I married a spirited, much older woman. Violette was amazing. Truly mesmerizing... and then at forty-five she gets pregnant with twins. I love my sons, but something has to give."

"I understand, Hot... I mean Jeremy."

He gives me a quizzical look as another voice

interrupts. I look up to see Eleanor.

Is everyone looking for a place to hide tonight?

Eleanor says, "Hey guys, Carter suggested that I find you, Jeremy. He said you seemed really tense and if you want, we can go in the other room, and he'll help your wife with the kids. I brought my table."

I can't disguise the horror on my face. This is getting ridiculous.

Her *table*? Declan is one thing. He's a single man. Even Austin. And Gaston.

But Jeremy is a married father with his wife and children in the other room.

Jeremy says, "I'm okay, thanks. Maybe tomorrow. I'll stop by your place. But honestly, I think Addison here could use your services."

Now my face is twisted like a corkscrew and I say, "Are you people insane?"

They both look like I slapped them, and Eleanor says, "Chill out, Addison. I think Jeremy is right. You should have come to me as soon as you got here. I should have offered when you were in the shop. You've been through a lot this week and massage therapy is so good for the mind, body, and spirit."

"Well, I don't need any... wait, what?" I shake my head to sort through the crazy and pull the sane bits to the forefront. "You're a massage therapist? You've been giving everyone *massages*?"

"Yes, of course. I just work in the shop to help out my sister when she's busy with her kids. But I'm a licensed therapist."

She pulls a card out of her bag and hands it to me. She takes my hands, which are sweaty, and she must be wondering what kind of nut gets this stressed out over a possible spa treatment.

"Addison, you deserve some pampering. Declan told me what he did, and it really seems like you guys aren't right for each other, but I hope you find love with Carter. I've never seen him look at anyone the way he looks at you." She squeezes my hands, pulls back and says, "I hope you aren't upset with me for spending time with Declan."

I can't possibly tell her what I was upset about because then I really will have to go home, and the idea of watching *The Muppets Take Manhattan* is sounding like a good escape from reality right now.

I reassure her that all is well, and we all leave the library. I even told her that maybe I would like a massage later. Why not, now that I know she isn't running a prostitution ring with the whole family?

Or at all.

Jeremy is the most reluctant to leave the peace of the library, but hopefully, his children have been pacified with some snacks and the movie has started. I would dim the lights and give them some blankets, too.

Hell, I would be happy to fall asleep with them if everyone would just shut the hell up. My nerves are shot and now there are cats happening tomorrow?

I can't go to a cat sanctuary, but maybe there's an outdoor option. I should sneak down to the scary room and see if I can find some Benadryl. I could take some for tomorrow and hand the rest out to the kids right now.

While I am ruminating on my great idea, I am stopped before I make it into the movie room. Jeremy was quick to move to his wife's side and Eleanor rushed back to Declan and the bourbon.

But Laura has a one-track mind and it's not her impending childbirth experience. She's had so many she probably just shoots them out like Pop Tarts out of the toaster.

I back up before she and her belly knock me over.

"Hi Laura, has the movie started?"

She pokes me in the chest, which she has to reach up to do, and says, "I've been silent this whole week because I figured you'd realize you don't belong here and leave, but I can see it's going to take more than what this family normally dishes out to get rid of you."

I'm really hoping she didn't grab the cheese knife off the buffet because if I have to wrestle a pregnant woman on Muppet movie night...

"Laura, I don't know what your problem is, but you have a husband... and a lovely... bunch of kids... and you're about to have another bundle... of joy. Your life is much better than mine. And don't you think Carter deserves some happiness?"

She balls up her little pudgy fists and screams, "What do you know about happiness, you big stupid bitch! You weren't at the prom. You didn't see what we could have had. And now I'm stuck with a boring sack of..."

Carter and the boring sack (otherwise known as Tyler) appear and Tyler says, "Laura, enough of this. I just got the kids settled and I will be goddamned if I have to do it again. Now get a hold of yourself. Addison, I'm so sorry. Her pregnancy hormones are just taking over her brain."

Hmm... I think it's different hormones of the more lust-filled variety, but I just nod and smile, grateful to be saved from the tiny round maniac.

Carter looks like he's ready to lose it... and I mean in a big way. His temples are throbbing, and his jaw looks like it's about to crack. If he had superpowers the house would be on fire.

But he gathers himself as he always seems to do and says, "Tyler, why don't you take Laura up to my room and let her lie down while the kids watch the movies? I'm sure they'll be fine now."

Tyler agrees and half drags a panting Laura towards the stairs.

We hear him as they mercifully disappear from sight, "Do you want to go into labor right now? This is not good for the baby, Laura. We talked about this. We don't want another preemie baby – you need to stay calm."

If he only knew what Camille was planning for the end of the week, he would take her out of town for the birth. If yelling at me has her this upset, wait until she finds out she's in love with her brother.

Carter pulls me into another hug and out of view of the movie room.

"I'm so sorry everyone is insane. Well, at least a lot of people. I thought this would be a fun diversion for you and I didn't think it through. Do you want me to take you back to Annapolis? I'll drive you or buy a plane ticket."

I look up at him and softly say, "Do you want me to go?"

He cups my face in his hands and says, "No, definitely not.

But I want you to be happy and not attacked. I promise I will keep Laura away from you for the rest of the week." He leans in closer to my ear and says, "Maybe you could come back to my room tonight?"

I turn and widen my eyes. "Laura's in your room."

"Not for long. Once these silly movies are over Tyler will be loading his entire sleeping family into the car and if he was smart, he would drive them to her mother's house and leave town. Maybe get a new identity."

I laugh and say, "I know, I think my sister could help him with that."

Carter squeezes my waist and takes my hands as we walk back toward the night's planned entertainment.

I feel a little nagging sense of responsibility for Tyler's mental health. Someone should tell him what's about to go down this week because Laura is going to need more than a little lie down to keep that baby in until it's ready to pop.

Episode 28
She Did WHAT?

"Are you sure you don't want to talk about it?"

I glance over at Carter, and he is gripping the steering wheel so tightly it may rip off any second. I should have offered to drive but this morning it seemed like the smartest thing to do was be quiet and get in the car.

Carter takes a deep breath and says, "No, I don't think so. What more is there to say?"

He has a point, but I persist. "You're right... but... maybe you should have skipped the cat sanctuary today. I'm sure your parents would understand."

"Well, my father doesn't know, and my mother only knows because she has a creepy sense of hearing and knows what's going on in every corner of the house at all times."

Note to self – leave that house sooner rather than later.

I look out the window at the passing horse farms and bucolic scenery and wish I was here under different circumstances.

Here are the current circumstances.

Last night Carter and I finally got a chance to sneak off to his room. The Muppet movies had long since ended and all the children were packed away in their beds... in their own houses... or so we thought.

I hadn't decided what I was going to do or not do

once we got to his room, but Carter has proven himself to be trustworthy and I wasn't afraid that he would pressure me to go further than I wanted.

Feeling more peaceful than I had in a while, even after the altercation with Laura, we reached the door of his room and I said, "Wait, do you think Laura was napping under or over the covers?"

Carter laughed and said, "I'm sure Tyler left her on top and she went under but she's fully clothed and she's not some kind of sicko."

We stared at each other for a moment and for a split second I thought of suggesting we head to my room instead, but he grabbed my hand and said, "I'm just joking. And besides I'm sure Caroline left a spare set of sheets in the room. She thinks of everything."

I knew he was right, so I nodded, and he opened the door to his room.

And I almost fell over him because he abruptly stopped in the doorway, his knees buckled, and he started screaming.

Even though I couldn't imagine what he was seeing to evoke such a reaction, I barreled past him into the room, solely running on adrenaline.

You tend to have these kinds of reactions when your naked, nine months pregnant half-sister is lying on your bed with her legs... oh my God... I can't even say it.

Thank God her stomach is so big that it eclipses all other body parts.

I turned to help Carter up once I realized Laura was not giving birth in the bed and in need of an ambulance, when Eleanor came running to the door, tossing her massage table to the ground in the hallway.

"What's going on in here?"

Her face was already white from fear of what she might find and then it turned into a gag when she saw what she saw.

What we all saw.

Eleanor scrunched up her face and said, "Oh my God, that thing is bigger than all the butts on the women in this family combined."

And it was so true – how many babies are in there?

You might wonder what Laura was doing while everyone was screaming.

A normal person, or even a semi-normal person, would rush to cover themselves in light of this audience.

But not the Pickle Queen.

She just lay there with a smug smile on her face while Carter crawled out of the room, and I slammed the door.

I heard voices in the room and realized that I left Eleanor in there.

And that's when Camille came flying down the hall.

There was so much yelling and freaking out that I am not even sure what happened next, but I know that someone retrieved Tyler from the guest room where he was lying down with his children because the little one got sick on too much candy and threw up in the middle of *Muppet Treasure Island*.

He didn't intend to fall asleep, and he assumed that Laura would be fine in Carter's room and that someone would come get him if Carter returned to his room before he brought Laura and the kids home.

You really can't blame the man. He is just trying to survive the crazy that is his life, and he doesn't understand the depths of Laura's obsession with Carter.

And of course, he also doesn't know that they are

brother and sister.

He thought all of our reactions were over the top and that we should be more forgiving. He said Laura probably just got hot and that none of us have been pregnant and didn't understand.

I think Carter had the same reaction that the younger pickle child had to the candy overindulgence, but his mother followed him into the bathroom, so I am not sure if the sight of his naked, pregnant sister made him throw up.

At least his hair is short so Camille didn't have to hold it back for him.

Laura needs professional help but hopefully, Tyler will keep her away from this family for the rest of the week... until they are summoned for the news.

As for Carter, Eleanor offered him an emergency massage, but he declined and went to bed.

I retreated to my own room but not before he found me and asked me to ride with him to the cat sanctuary today.

I really thought the events of the evening would be enough to cancel this activity, but Camille is keeping this incident quiet and she slipped me some allergy pills and another apparatus to aid me today.

These people just get weirder all the time.

Carter rubs his face while we are stopped at a light and says, "Look, Addison, I would understand if you wanted to go home and pretend you never met me."

The light turns green and he pulls into the parking lot of the cat rescue organization.

I didn't realize we were already here. I have spent the whole ride thinking about last night and haven't even considered the fresh hell that awaits me now.

But that's okay because Camille has me all prepared and protected from stray cat hairs flying into my eyes.

I lean over and give Carter an awkward hug whether he wants one or not.

"I don't want to go home. It is a bit of a challenge here and more than I expected, but I'm here with you."

I pull back and see he is finally almost smiling.

"And besides, where would I get a pair of these at home *and* the chance to let cats crawl all over me?"

He laughs and says, "It does feel like a once-in-a-lifetime opportunity."

I pop my new science class goggles on my head and try not to think about the fact that Camille brought these up from the basement.

You know what goes on down there.

It seems like overkill, but I don't want puffy eyes. I need to be on the lookout for more sightings of an unpleasant nature, unless Laura has already gone into labor and is in the hospital.

Episode 29
Family Pride

"Sweetie, if the kitten keeps attacking your hair, I can't braid it."

This is the first time someone has said that to me.

Also, it is the first time a man with long blond hair sporting a rose tattoo on his cheek and wearing black eyeliner has ever spoken to me.

Caroline says, "I'll hold the little guy and then he can go back to his mama when it's Aunt Caroline's turn for rainbow hair braiding."

I hand the adorable black kitten over to Caroline and take a deep cleansing breath.

Yes, I am at the Pride event in honor of you guessed it... Uncle Bernard.

But that was expected as I previously mentioned that an elaborate Pride festival was going to be Friday's funeral event.

What I didn't expect was that at the cat sanctuary yesterday I would become a mother.

No, Carter did not impregnate me in the "get to know your new cat" room.

Yes, they have that for people who want to see if the cat they have chosen will like them or claws their faces off.

But no, I didn't need to go to that room at all because, from the moment I entered the cat asylum, I mean sanctuary, a little black fur ball glued himself to me like Velcro.

I tried very hard to resist. I kept peeling him off me and handing him to other people.

However, he always found his way back to me.

I took off the ridiculous goggles once I got inside because there were people there other than the family, and the volunteers were giving me odd looks.

I guess most people who think they are allergic to cats just stay home instead of wearing hazmat gear.

I know I said I was allergic to cats, but the funny thing was that I felt fine in there and had no allergy symptoms at all.

Camille did give me an allergy pill before we left the house, but an over-the-counter medication isn't normally going to completely erase a severe pet allergy, only make it tolerable for short exposures.

I was worried that Carter would think I lied about my problem, and I was being overly dramatic.

Obviously, it goes without saying that this man doesn't need any more unnecessary drama in his life.

So, I did the only sensible thing a girl could do in this situation.

I called my mother.

I hesitated for a few minutes because I hadn't talked to my parents since I'd been here, and even though I'm sure Erica gave them a good summary of recent events, she was going to want to talk about more than my cat allergies.

I managed to peel the kitten off me and hand it to Caroline long enough to step outside with my phone.

Mom answered on the first ring.

"Well, it's about time we heard from you."

"Hi Mom, sorry, it's been a lot."

She huffed loudly and said, "Yes, your sister informed us that you've broken up with Declan, and you are unemployed and living in a haunted mansion with rich people in Tennessee. Honestly, Addison, I don't know what to make of it."

I wrinkled my brows and said, "I'm in Kentucky... and the house isn't haunted... at least I don't think so... it's a long story, Mom. And I promise I'll call back and give you more details, but for now, I have an important question."

She sighed and said, "I can't wait to hear."

"Am I allergic to cats?"

She said, "What? No, you're not allergic to cats. Only horses. When we took you to the allergist the horsehair bump on your test was as big as my thumb and don't you remember that's why you couldn't go to that snooty kid Rebecca's birthday party in sixth grade? She had pony rides."

I was so confused.

"I do remember going to the allergist and you told me I was also allergic to dogs and cats when we got home."

I could hear her silent wheels turning to figure out how to get out of this one.

"Well, if you must know, I just told you that because you and your sister were always bugging us for a pet and that bastard father of yours hates animals and wouldn't let you have one. I figured if you thought you were allergic, you'd let it go."

I shook my head to knock out the crazy and said, "So you lied to me? What if I had wanted a pet when I was grown? And why are you calling Dad a bastard? That's a little harsh. Lots of people don't want pets in the house."

I didn't add that my parents aren't the best housekeepers, and we would have been buried in fur and that's probably why my father didn't want to deal with it.

"Addison, I can't talk right now. You just call me out of the blue after how long with this silly question and you have no idea what's going on with us, let alone do you share why your life is in a dumpster... so call me back when you have time to talk. Now be careful of the ghosts and stay away from black cats."

Carter found me outside at that moment with my mouth hanging open and a small black cat crying in his arms.

"Addison, I think this cat knows you from a past life or something. Well, I don't really believe that but Caroline suggested it and it's starting to make sense." He handed me the little whiny baby and he instantly calmed down.

I wish I could say the same for myself.

Carter noticed my pained expression and said, "Hey, are you okay?"

I told him about the strange conversation with my mom.

"Do you think they're having problems? Or maybe your mother is just trying to make you feel guilty for not calling. Mothers do that. I mean, mine doesn't, but as you can see my family is not representative of cultural norms."

He did get me to smile and agree that she is just worried about me and that I will call her back and everything is probably fine.

For all I know, she may have been annoyed that Dad

left his muddy shoes in the hallway again right before I called. It doesn't take much to set her off.

We went back inside and in an insanely impulsive moment, I decided to adopt the kitten, even though I am technically homeless and most definitely unemployed.

Caroline and Camille both assured me that if I didn't want to keep the cat long term they would keep it at the house.

This made me feel better, and honestly, with everything going on in my life I could use an emotional support animal.

Only now I realize that kittens are maniacs, and even though this one is adorable in his rainbow bandana, I am not sure how I am going to deal with his behavior.

He seems a little calmer sitting on Caroline's lap, but that's not surprising. She has very Zen energy.

"So, what are you going to name this little guy?"

The hairdresser, whose name is Greg, says, "Why don't you name him Bernard? After all, it's because of that absolute icon of the Lexington gay community that we've all come together."

Hmm... he's not wrong.

"That's a great idea, but what if Laura names her baby Bernard? She'll be so mad if there's a cat running around here with the same name."

Laura did go into labor after all, but not right after the "incident" as we are now calling it.

Peter called yesterday to let the family know that his sister was at the hospital, and even though she was a little early the baby boy was healthy and weighed over nine pounds.

I wasn't surprised by that, and I wanted to ask if they were sure there wasn't another one in there.

Laura is fine – apparently, the more babies you have the more they shoot out like a toddler on the slip and slide.

Caroline laughs and says, "She isn't going to name her son Bernard and you can call this little guy Bernie. How cute is that? And besides, after this weekend Laura is going to have a lot more to worry about than her child sharing a name with a cat."

Greg's eyes widen and he says, "Ohhh, is there tea? Please spill, I haven't heard any gossip in a long time."

Carter appears at my side and says, "Is this lovely lady's hair done yet? I was thinking of taking her on an afternoon paddle boat ride on the pond. And the little fur ball, too, of course."

Since there isn't a private road to do a parade, the event is set up more like a church festival with booths of food and games, the pond is decorated with a pride banner, and they brought in little brightly colored paddle boats.

Except a quick glance would tell you this isn't a church event, especially when you spot the guy with the assless chaps and The Village People leading the dancing.

The guys are definitely bringing people together in fellowship, though. Of all people, Declan is out there with Eleanor doing the YMCA moves with his whole heart.

Of course, the bourbon is flowing too, but I think my ex is evolving.

"Yep, she's all done, and her hair is 'pridetastic.' Okay, Caroline, you're next. Let's talk about that tea."

Carter gives me a quizzical look, but I wave it off and pretend that I am distracted by little Bernie's tiny paws. I actually am because they are soft and precious and need to be smooched, but I also don't want to tell Carter that a relative stranger is now going to try to pry his parents' long-held secret from Caroline.

I'm not worried, though. She has guarded the secret for many years, and there is plenty of public gossip about this family that she can dish before the full buffet hits the streets.

Then Greg can have all the tea in Lexington.

Episode 30
It's Almost Over

"Where have you been?"

As soon as I blurted that out, I remembered I have no claim on Carter or right to know what he's been doing all day, and I did see him at lunch.

I've been hiding... I mean hanging out in my room because I am getting increasingly anxious about this week's grand finale.

But I can't say that because it's not my family that is about to take a big hit.

"I'm sorry, that came out wrong. Let's start over. Hello Carter, it's so nice of you to drop by my room. Is it almost time for the basketball game?"

He smiles and hands me a shopping bag.

"I was just talking to my mother about... well you know... and she gave me this t-shirt for you to wear tonight."

I take the bag and step out of the way so Carter can come in.

I pull tonight's uniform out of the bag and it's a Kentucky Wildcats shirt.

"At least it's not black, and royal blue looks good on white girls with red hair." I hold it up to my body in the light of the bedside lamp.

He closes the distance between us, gently takes the shirt out of my hands, and kisses my lips and then my head, followed by a strong embrace.

"You look good in everything. I'm sorry I brought you into this whole mess, but I can't tell you how grateful I am to have you here. I often feel alone in my family, and now... it's about to get harder."

I talk into his shoulder because I don't want to let go yet.

"So, tomorrow is still the day?"

"Yes."

"What about Laura? Is she out of the hospital?"

I just can't believe they are going to spring this on her right after getting home with a new baby, but many things this week have shocked me so who knows?

He gently pulls out of our hug and sits down on my bed. I join him and he says, "Normally she would be, but rich people can stay in the hospital longer if they want to and apparently Laura takes full advantage of her privilege. But it's a good thing. Tyler was told by his in-laws that they were coming home and that they needed Tyler to attend a family meeting."

"Does he know it's a joint meeting with your family? That would be suspicious."

"No, I think they gave him as little information as possible, and Peter isn't coming tonight so we don't have to worry about saying anything to Scarlet and Austin, because my mother also told them *we* are having a family meeting."

"What a mess. Do you think Tyler will tell Laura right away?"

"He's her husband and it's up to him. But my mother refuses to wait. She said Laura is always pregnant or recovering from childbirth, and they can't put it off any longer, especially now that Laura's behavior towards me has gotten even more reckless."

I massage my temples and say, "She's going to need a good therapist. Honestly, everyone will. I know one thing – I wouldn't want to be Tyler – what a thing to have to tell his wife."

Carter is quiet and opens his mouth to say something and then closes it again. I figure if I wait long enough, he'll say it.

"Are you going to leave tomorrow before the meeting or will you come with me, and wait for me?"

"If you want me to be there, I'll be there. But I am still not sure it's the right thing to do. I am not family and I've been in your life for a week. How do your parents feel about it?"

"I don't care. I need an ally in that room, and I want it to be you. I know we hardly know each other but I feel like the events of this week have sped up the process. And I want the chance to get to know you. I promise you we will get out of here as soon as possible after it's over."

"I'll be there but I am not saying one peep. Maybe no one will notice me."

He pulls a stray lock of hair out of my face and touches my cheek. "I'll know you're there. Now let's get ready for this basketball game and get this over with."

I smile and get up to change my shirt. I was going to do it in front of Carter, but it feels like we've moved on from the intimate moment and I need the bathroom anyway.

While I'm there he says, "Hey, did you call your mother back today?"

I call out, "I did, but she didn't answer, which is weird."

I put my hair up into a ponytail and come back out into the bedroom.

"I'm sure everything is fine. They were probably at the farmer's market or whatever they do for fun on weekends."

It just occurred to me that I don't know what my parents do when they're not working. I left home and didn't ever really connect with them as an adult.

Well, this is my chance to change all of that. It can be part of all the many changes going on, and if I can support Carter maybe he can help me too, and we can see if this thing will go anywhere.

"Are you ready? Scarlet just texted me that they are all waiting for us downstairs."

I smile and he takes my hand.

"Think of it this way – it's almost over."

I know he's talking about tomorrow more than tonight but at least this is the grand finale of the funeral week.

If I end up joining this family, I hope Dominique lives to be one hundred because I need recovery time from this experience.

It's a good long walk back to the entryway in this house, which gives me some time to adjust my attitude to one of fun and frivolity and leave the worries from our conversation in my room.

As soon as we reach the assembled family members, Scarlet grabs me away from Carter.

"Hey, are you okay?"

I blink a few times and can't think of a reason she would be asking that question.

"Sure, I'm fine. Why do you ask?"

She widens her eyes and says in a low voice, "My mother told me about what happened with Laura the other night. She didn't want to, but I dragged it out of her after I heard Uncle Gaston telling Grandma Dominique that he heard screaming coming from Carter's room. As much as I hoped it was screaming of the good variety, I figured it wasn't."

I clear my throat and look around to see if anyone is watching us in serious conversation, but they are all distracted with their own stuff.

"It was traumatic for Carter."

Scarlet wrinkles her face and says, "Well, that's a little dramatic, don't you think? It was just a naked pregnant woman. It's not like she was dead, and I really think he's seen Laura naked at some point in all these years."

Why did I have to say it was traumatic? Can't I learn to laugh things off?

Scarlet gets that skeptical look on her face and says, "You're not jealous, are you?"

"Oh no, not at all. I just felt bad for Laura. And Carter. And everyone involved."

"I hear you, it is sad that she can't stop this obsession." Scarlet pulls a pack of gum out of her purse and offers me a piece. "So how did Tyler manage to get her out of there? What did he say? That must have been the very definition of awkward."

Before I get a chance to answer we are called to attention to depart for the game and the spreading of Bernard's ashes.

Now I can stop worrying about having a good reason to look distressed because I think by now everyone knows that I think it's odd and also impossible to scatter ashes at a university basketball stadium during a March Madness game.

But knowing this family they will find a way, even

though it may end up being illegal, inappropriate, and completely off the wall.

Episode 31
Oopsie

Our caravan is greeted outside the stadium by Don, who is some kind of concierge or host that deals with important fans and patrons of the school.

I don't know if anyone in the family attended this college, but I am sure they have supported the school financially in some capacity.

But is that enough to let rich people show up with a dead guy in a jar?

I guess we will find out.

Don explains that he is going to escort us to our special family viewing box and that Mister Bernard will be honored with a moment of silence before the game starts.

"However, I must remind you that you can't throw the ashes on the court then because-"

"People will end up with ashes in their beer." Austin finishes the absurd sentence for Don.

Everyone nods in agreement.

They can't do it then? Does that mean they can do it later?

We haven't seen Austin in days. With all the drama, I forgot he was missing. I guess he was pressured into showing up for the last day of the funeral... or he just really likes basketball.

He doesn't look happy to be here, though. Maybe he was hoping to get away for the weekend and Camille told him he had to stay put for the meeting tomorrow.

Come to think of it I can't believe Scarlet didn't ask me if I knew anything about that. I need to stay near Carter tonight so no one else can question me.

Apparently, the senior Partons have arrived back in town now and they are with Laura at the hospital. Camille is showing everyone the photos.

I wonder how that's working out. I know a new baby is a huge distraction, but did Tyler tell Laura about the meeting?

There are so many people hiding things from so many people I can't keep it straight.

I will stop worrying about who knows what and just assume my position as Carter's emotional support person and mind my own business.

Then we can get away and give him some space from his family and maybe I can start working on my next move since I am homeless and unemployed and the mother of a kitten.

Carter has also hinted that he's thinking of quitting the family business, which he mentioned to me quietly at lunch when I asked him if he could take all this time off from work.

I hope his parents won't blame me for that, but if they do, they do. They should be self-aware enough to know that Carter needs some space from this situation.

Crap, I stopped listening to Don and wandered off to Carter's side and now I don't know if he announced the actual plan for scattering the ashes.

It may be best if I don't know. I'll just stay away from the urn so that no matter what, there is no chance of coming into contact with any part of Uncle Bernard.

I was reading disturbing stories about ash

scatterings gone wrong and if they blew into my face and got stuck to my lipstick, I don't know how I would prevent myself from making a scene.

Yes, I read that it happens and therefore I am not even wearing lip balm.

We're indoors but you never know when someone might turn a fan on and your makeup routine turns into a horror show.

Sometimes there are still bone fragments in the ashes and ugh... I have to stop thinking about this.

Carter is still holding my hand as he guides me into the luxury seating area.

It's just the immediate family and no kids. Violette and her brood didn't come.

And thankfully Declan and Eleanor left for Annapolis this morning. It wasn't so terrible that he stayed but it was starting to get weird, even for this family.

The box is high in the sky as promised, and well stocked with food and drink. The seating looks super comfortable, and we have all the amenities one would expect.

There is even a special pedestal table set up for Bernard's urn, and I'm glad so I know exactly where to sit on the opposite side of the room. It's not like I could yell out, "Hey who has the ashes?" and then run in the other direction.

Dominique and her huge purse are sitting closer to the urn than I would allow, but it's not my call. Hopefully, she will stay sober enough that Bernard won't need to be swept up before he's scattered.

Basketball isn't really my thing, but the crowd is hyped and in a moment my spirits are raised by the infectious energy in the building. Carter brings me a glass of wine, and we sit down with Scarlet, Tim, and Austin.

I wonder if Tim is invited to the family meeting. Probably not because Scarlet either doesn't know about it or doesn't know she needs support.

The crowd starts to quiet down, and the announcer begins introducing the game and we have our moment of silence for Bernard.

Okay, this feels pretty normal, and I can forget about tomorrow and just try to enjoy tonight.

I can't believe Dominique is using this time to root around in her purse. Maybe she's a little deaf and doesn't realize that we are supposed to show respect for the dearly departed right now. Wait... what is she doing?

She brought her own snacks in a baggie with all this food here?

I try to see what she has in her purse without being too obvious. It could be medicine that she has to take at a certain time.

But it looks like dirt. Maybe it's granola or seeds or... oh my God.

She glances at Camille and nods and then before anyone can stop her, she sprinkles the contents of the baggie onto the court.

Except ashes don't weigh a whole lot so they are now deposited on the heads of the couple below us.

"Ow, what the hell was that?"

The woman touches her head and looks around.

Her equally confused husband says, "What I didn't feel anything. Maybe somebody's throwing confetti."

"Do you see any confetti? There's some kind of dirt on my head and something hard hit me."

Dominique peers into the almost empty baggie and says to no one in particular, "Well, son of a bitch, there's bones in here."

She looks at her daughter and says, "I think I just beaned that woman with a finger or a toe."

That now wins the award for the least likely sentence I ever thought I'd hear.

Episode 32
The Meeting

It's not easy to get the images from last night out of my mind.

After Dominique took quite a scolding from her daughter and son-in-law, the mood shifted.

Apparently, Dominique thought she had gotten permission from Camille to drop some of Bernard's ashes on the heads of unsuspecting basketball fans, but in reality, her daughter's look meant, "What the fuck are you doing?"

Easy mistake to make, right?

In her defense, Dominique is old, and the elderly and little kids seem to get away with all sorts of bad behavior, especially in this family.

Carter took me aside toward the end of the game and told me that a decision had been made to scatter the rest of Bernard's ashes on the school grounds, but only his parents were going to do it as a crowd would draw unwanted attention.

I thought Don had outlined a better plan, but since I didn't listen to it and I was eager for this insanity to end, I just nodded my head.

As the funeral week drew to a close, I was relieved. There is a reason that this tradition hasn't caught on and most families don't choose to celebrate funeral weeks that are orchestrated like activities on a cruise ship.

Although Violette's job at the family firm is to plan

funerals, it sounds like she is convincing more and more people to indulge in this experience.

I don't know if it's healthy or not. Maybe I'm the weirdo and this is all perfectly normal.

Speaking of perfectly normal, I am now in my room on a Sunday morning, packing up my things and deciding on the right outfit for a meeting where my maybe, possibly, soon-to-be boyfriend's parents announce that they are in a polyamorous relationship with their best friends and all of the kids are half-siblings because Franklin Parton's guys can't swim.

Business casual?

The knock on my door signals that it's time to go. I pull the basic navy-blue t-shirt over my head and zip my jeans.

I will go with Carter and lend my support, but I am going as regular Addison, not in a uniform mandated by anyone.

I take a deep breath and remember that in a few short hours, Carter and I will be on the road to the airport and a tranquility spa resort in Sedona.

It will feel quite the opposite of this "vacation."

"I'm coming, hold on."

I finish attaching the clasp to my second earring and peer down at my phone before popping it into my mini backpack.

Yes, I am bringing a purse downstairs, just in case I need to get out at a moment's notice, I'll have all my essentials on me.

Crap, it looks like my mother called while I was in the shower.

I don't have the time or mental capacity to call her back now. I'll call her when we get to the airport. That way if she starts yelling at me for continuing this great escape from reality with a near stranger, I can pretend they are calling our flight, or I lost the phone signal.

I open the door to an ashen-faced Carter.

"Hey, you look like somebody died. I mean, somebody new died. I mean, a different person. Are you okay?"

He rubs his face vigorously with both hands and says, "Any better? My blood isn't flowing normally this morning. I didn't sleep much. Let's just get this over with."

I wrap him in a big hug, and he feels as stiff as he looks.

I hope he's not going to fall apart because I don't know what I'll do. And what other support person does he have? His whole family is about to take a big hit, and I don't even know if he has a best friend I can call.

Ugh... there was a time when Laura would have claimed to be his best friend.

I shudder like I've seen a ghost thinking of Laura. As we turn the corner to the hallway where we are meeting in the library, I think of how grateful I am that she is privileged enough for a longer maternity stay.

It may be selfish for everyone to expect Tyler to deal with this, but he is going to be the most affected by this news, no matter how or when all the parents choose to share it.

The chatter from the room is lower than usual, and I don't know if that means they are tired from the week, or they are whispering among themselves speculating on the reason for this meeting.

Carter takes my hand and surveys the room. There are two empty seats next to Scarlet and Austin, and I know that's where we are headed.

Peter and Tyer are on the other side.

It's like battle lines have been drawn, but no one knows why.

Although, if anyone should be on the other side of a fortification, it is the four people seated in the center of the room.

Claude and Camille LeMieux, and Franklin and Eloise Parton.

The Partons look like any older, middle-aged couple who just came back from a long vacation.

Tanned, smiling, and wealthy.

They are either delusional or excellent actors if they think this is going to go well.

Seated next to Camille are her mother and Caroline.

Dominique is muttering about getting people up on a Sunday for this nonsense.

I wonder if she knows.

And in the back of the room, Uncle Gaston is pacing and whispering into a phone.

Scarlet leans over to us and says, "So what do you think you're getting?"

Carter looks even whiter now and says, "What? What would I be getting?"

Do they normally give out prizes in this family when they deliver bad news, like Oprah? – "Sorry kids, we are all banging each other, and Claude fathered the whole bunch of you, but look under your seat for keys to your new car!"

I'm so glad we have a flight booked now so that we have an excuse to get out of here.

I know that sounds insensitive, but Carter wants to go, and I don't blame him. It will come out that he's known for almost fifteen years, and he hid it from everyone.

That is likely to go over as well as a dead guy's ashes on someone's head at a basketball game.

Scarlet rolls her eyes and says, "It's Bernard's Will reading. I know none of us need more money, but I'm sure he left us all something of sentimental value."

Austin says, "I wouldn't be surprised if he left everything to the cats and the gays and we are wasting time when we could be doing... well, anything but sitting here."

I swallow and manage a weak smile.

Were they told this was the Will reading, or did they just assume it?

It is a logical assumption given it is the wrap-up of the funeral week and Bernard was a wealthy man with no children.

Camille starts clapping her hands like a kindergarten teacher to call the room to order.

I suddenly feel sick and self-conscious, as if Carter and I are guilty of something. No one else looks like they are going to throw up on the Persian rug.

The other men mostly look bored (Austin), anxious (Tyler), or confused (Peter).

And the "dads" look like they are thrilled that Camille is the leader of their little quartet.

I glance around the room for an ally and my eyes settle on Caroline's.

She starts inhaling and exhaling deeply, which I know is to remind me to get centered by focusing on my breath.

Perhaps Carter and I have been a little selfish because he isn't the only one who knew this secret and kept it, although Caroline was basically being blackmailed.

Pretty soon I will be breathing deeply in the Sedona desert and looking at the big rocks. Maybe in a mud bath with a sparkling drink.

No wonder I don't want to talk to my mother and get a dose of reality.

Luckily Caroline is keeping Bernie, the kitten, until I get home and settle somewhere.

Everyone is quiet now and Camille has the floor.

I notice that Tyler has his phone on his lap and is texting.

I can't help but wonder if he told Laura what he was doing this morning, but the Will reading excuse is perfectly plausible and Uncle Bernard probably did leave something to the Partons.

Camille sits back down and rubs her hands along her linen pants.

"Thank you all for coming this morning, and for being here all week to honor Bernard. He loved all of you and he has left something in his Will to every one of you, including charities that were close to his heart, such as the cat sanctuary and the local organization to help LGBTQ teens."

Austin smirked as if to say, "Called it," but I know he doesn't care about the money and he isn't anti-cat or homophobic. He's just anxious to go wherever it was he wanted to be this weekend.

Everyone shares their support and a few even clap for Bernard's generosity.

I notice Eloise is especially enthusiastic as if she was just brought onstage at a Springsteen concert.

I hate to break it to her, but no amount of positivity

is going to help with what's coming.

Unless... no, that's ridiculous.

For a split second, I imagined that maybe I was projecting my own feelings, and everyone would accept this news and all will be well.

After all, this is not a traditional family.

Or maybe I am as delusional as Eloise.

Franklin is starting to look like he needs the bathroom and I just noticed that Claude is wearing the same clothes he wore last night.

Never mind, they're all hanging on by a thread.

Camille regains the floor and says, "We are going to do the Will reading next week when the family attorney, Mr. Blackwell, is back from the Cayman Islands."

Dominique huffs and grabs her cane. "Well, why didn't you say so? What in heaven's name are we doing here now?"

Camille turns to her mother with a tight smile. "We have other news, now that the Partons are home."

She smiles at her partners (I guess that's the right word) and squeezes Eloise's hand.

Scarlet turns a shade reminiscent of her name and gasps, "Oh no, does someone have cancer?"

Camille shakes her head and says, "Oh no, nothing like that."

She looks at the other three in her relationship and they all nod in unison.

"How many of you know about polyamorous relationships?"

Austin rolls his eyes. "Seriously, Mom. Someone is coming out of the closet, and we need a family meeting for that. In this family?"

Scarlet adds, "Austin, polyamorous people can be

gay or straight, but I have to agree, Mom. If someone has something personal to share, they can freely do it with all of us at any time. It doesn't have to be a big deal. Uncle Bernard wouldn't want us to be judgmental."

Peter says, "And I don't know why we're here at all." He points to himself, Tyler, and his parents.

His eyes widen like a cartoon rodent's, and he says, "Please don't tell me it's Tyler, Laura, and Carter."

Now all eyes are on me, and I wish there *was* a closet readily available.

I would gladly lock myself in, even if the closet was full of real rodents.

Episode 33
Nothing Left But the Shrieking

"Well, all I can say is couldn't you have waited until I was dead to tell me this?"

Dominique is unsteadily on her feet and luckily for everyone involved, her cane is needed to hold her upright and can't be used as a weapon of mass destruction.

The room is silent except for Austin's laughter and Eloise's crying.

And we haven't even gotten to the whole story.

So far Camille has explained that the two couples have been involved in a four-way since their honeymoons.

Uncle Gaston looks up from his phone, wrinkles his face, and says, "What the hell are you going on about? I'm going golfing."

I suppose leaving is better than staying and making things worse.

Austin wipes his eyes and says, "Mom, stop, this is so ridiculous. You expect us to believe that you and... that Dad and..." He looks at Franklin who now appears to be ready to be embalmed in the basement.

Scarlet has her head between her legs and pops up and says, "Austin, do you really think this is a joke? April Fool's isn't for a couple of weeks. And does anyone look like this is funny?"

Austin opens his mouth but nothing comes out.

Tyler is still fiddling with his phone and Peter is on his feet.

"The old lady is right. Sorry, Mrs. Dumas." He runs his fingers through his hair and says, "Why do any of us need to know this?"

Caroline clears her throat and says, "Peter, Dominique, please sit down. And Austin, your sister is right. Please take this seriously. Camille has more to tell you."

Peter is still on his feet and now he's pacing. "How are you involved in this? What did you do, cast a sex spell on everyone? And Carter, why are you sitting there like you lost your voice." He stares at Carter, and he grips my hand harder. "Oh, I get it. You knew about this."

Carter shifts in his seat and says, "Just let my mother finish the story, Peter. Save your outrage."

Peter exhales a huge breath and sits back down. He glances at his parents and seems to be grasping the significance of this conversation.

Camille sits down and folds her hands in her lap.

Honestly, I don't know how she is doing this. But of course, she also cuts dead people open, so she is tougher than me.

Camille's eyes are glassy, and I know she's holding back tears. "There is no easy way to say this, so I won't delay or sugarcoat it any longer." She glances at each of her children and at Peter and even Tyler.

"Franklin was unable to have children. So, because of our relationship arrangement, we all decided that Claude would father Eloise's children so they could have a family, too. Peter and Laura are Claude's children."

Scarlet gasps and says, "What do you mean? Are you

saying..."

Claude finally decides to help out as more than a sperm donor and adds, "Yes, Scarlet. You, Carter, and Austin are the half-siblings of Peter and Laura, who are also my biological children."

Dominique falls back into her chair and Caroline rushes over to steady her.

Austin's mouth is hanging open wide enough to shove a grapefruit in there, and Scarlet is gripping the arm of her chair.

Peter's face is an unnatural shade of green and he's shaking.

But the real problem is the shrieking coming from the phone on Tyler's knee.

Tyler grabs the phone and says, "Laura, honey, I had no idea. I thought they were trying to have a secret meeting without you and didn't want to let them get away with it."

Carter leaps to his feet. "Did you come in here with Laura on speakerphone from her hospital bed? How stupid can you be?"

Tyler is in his face and practically spitting. "I'm the stupid one? My wife just gave birth and all of you assholes decide this is the time for sharing family secrets?"

He looks at his in-laws and points his finger, "I thought you came home to see your new grandchild, but no, you just missed banging your friends over here and you let this woman decide that now was the time to traumatize your daughter."

Franklin says, "Please, Tyler. We wanted you to decide when to break it to her. That's why we did this while she was in the hospital. We know Laura has been unstable for years because of... well, you know."

Tyler takes the phone off speaker and says, "Laura, I am so sorry. Yes, I'm coming right now. No, I won't let anyone come with me. Don't worry."

He throws his phone down and says, "I do know why Laura has been unstable for years. She's been in love with her half-brother."

Carter says, "Tyler, she didn't know that, and I tried to dissuade her."

All eyes are on Carter now.

Scarlet says, "Carter, please tell me that you didn't know about this. Tyler is just upset for Laura, but you didn't know your sister has had a massive crush on you your whole life?"

Carter sits down and cradles his head in his hands. I move to hug him and all of a sudden Tyler is on top of us and everyone is yelling and here comes Dominique with the cane.

"Get off of him right now. This boy didn't do anything to you. Go to that hospital right now and take care of your wife."

Tyler adjusts his rumpled clothes and Carter stands up with me behind him.

I guess I should be glad they only whip out wooden weapons in this family, instead of guns or knives.

Tyler says, "Fine, but this isn't over."

He glares at his in-laws and storms out of the room.

Peter covers his eyes like a toddler watching a scary movie and follows his brother-in-law.

Caroline sighs and says, "That could have gone better, but at least no one died."

The last thing this family needs is another funeral.

My phone ringing breaks the silence and it's my

mother.

I no sooner get the phone to my ear (I just wanted to tell her I will call her back in a few minutes) when I hear screaming and dishes breaking.

"And you can stay out there in the alley for all I care!"

That was so loud I think most of the people in the room heard it.

Eager for a distraction from their own drama, everyone seems fixated on mine.

"Mom, what is going on? Are you okay?"

"You know what's going on? I would tell you, but you never take my calls because you're off gallivanting in fantasy land while your parents are falling apart up here."

"What do you mean? Is somebody sick?"

This is getting embarrassing, which is really saying something after recent events in this room.

"Oh, someone is sick all right. Me! I am sick of your father's bullshit, and if you don't come home soon and intervene... I said I don't care if you pitch a tent on the lawn!"

"Mom, did you call Erica?"

My parents have never fought like this. At least I don't think they have.

"Oh, your sister is off on some saving-the-world mission to parts unknown so it's just me here dealing with this all on my own."

I look at Carter and his eyes are full of genuine concern, despite his own family's shitstorm.

I hope he is understanding when I tell him that Sedona is off. I can't possibly go on a fun adventure now.

"Okay, Mom I will be there. I'll get a flight. I'll figure it out. Just don't do anything crazy. Why don't you go to a friend's house."

I finally calm her down enough to get off the phone and all eyes are on me.

"I'm so sorry about that. It seems I have my own family issues to attend to so thank you all for a... nice week... and your hospitality."

Camille walks over and puts an arm around my shoulder. "It's okay, Addison. Thanks for being here today for Carter. And let us know if there is anything you need."

Everyone in the room echoes the sentiment and Dominique pulls out her checkbook. Before I have a chance to tell her I don't need money, Carter says, "So I guess Sedona is off?"

Scarlet says, "You knew what we were going to hear today, and you planned a vacation?"

Claude says, "That's enough. There will be plenty of time to process what happened here today, but your brother has taken on the worst of it. You, of all people, should understand. You want to be a therapist. People have more problems than breaking up with their boyfriends or losing social media followers."

Austin begins to steer his sister out of the room. "Dad, that's not fair. Scarlet isn't that shallow. She's just in shock. But I am that shallow, so I am taking her to find Tim and then I am out of here for a while."

The Partons excuse themselves and Camille and Claude walk them out.

Caroline says, "I'm going to check on little Bernie." She stares intently at me and at Carter.

"You should both do what is best for you. As you can see, everyone here has done the same."

Dominique starts to stand again, and Caroline

moves to her aid.

As she walks a little more steadily towards the door, she says, "Addison, I want you to have this for your trip."

"Oh, Mrs. Dumas, I couldn't take your money. I'll be fine."

Carter takes the check from his grandmother and tucks it into her purse. "Thank you, Grandma, but I'll take care of Addison."

She smiles and says, "I think you'll take care of each other."

They leave and it's just me and Carter in what could be our final moments together.

He leans down, kisses me softly, and says, "I just need to go back to my place before we go to the airport."

I sigh and say, "I can't go to Sedona. My family needs me. I thought you would understand."

"Oh, I do understand. It just snowed in Michigan, and I am not packed for the right season."

My breath catches in my throat. "You're coming to Michigan? To help me deal with this mess after everything you've been through this week?"

"Addison, you just sat beside me through the hardest thing I have ever had to go through. I can handle a marital spat. You'll see – we'll all be laughing together on your parents' couch in a week and making snow angels in the yard."

I squeeze his hand in thanks as he heads over to his cottage to pack.

The only problem with his plan is that our yard is small and my Dad may be sleeping in a tent in the snow angel-making area.

And from the tone of my mother's voice, the only person shrieking louder than her is Laura.

Oh well.

Carter can handle the drama and I'm sure my mother is overreacting.

What could possibly go wrong that is any worse than what happened here today?

Maybe we should pack some bourbon and Dominique's cane, just in case.

Start reading The Parent Feud, Book Two in the Meet the Parents series on Kindle Vella:

https://www.amazon.com/kindle-vella/story/B0C17V15TY

Addison's story continues as she heads to Michigan to deal with HER family, with her maybe soon-to-be boyfriend, Carter, along for the ride.

Also coming soon to Kindle Unlimited as a full length sequel, but can read it as I write it on Kindle Vella!

Novels by Carol Maloney Scott

Fun Feminine Fiction
Rom-Com on the Edge Series
Dazed & Divorced (Book 1)
There Are No Men (Book 2)
Afraid of Her Shadow (Book 3)
The Juggling Act (Book 4)
Accidental Makeovers (Book 5)
Let's Hear it From the Boys (A Short Story Collection)

Love Pixies Series
Love Pixies (Book 1)

Spooky Matchmakers Series
Nobody Tells Lia Anything (Book 1)
Something Molly Can't See (Book 2)

Adventures of City Girl Series
Adventures of City Girl Season One

Kindle Vella Stories by Carol Maloney Scott
https://linktr.ee/cmscottauthor

Click on my Linktree above to read all of my Kindle Vella stories, including the sequel to this story in progress, The Parent Feud!

The first 10 episodes of all Vella stories are FREE and you can easily read on your phone tablet or any device – no subscription or special device needed!

Join Me On The Edge

Click here to become an Edgy Reader and receive a FREE BOOK as my thank you for joining!

The fun doesn't stop with the FREE DOWNLOAD!

As a member of my Edgy Readers Group, you will receive:
- More free books!
- News on upcoming releases!
- Exclusive contests and giveaways!
- Updates on projects and new series in the works!
- Polls asking for your opinion!
- Shenanigans!
- Wiener dog pictures!
- Excerpts!

I can't wait for YOU to join the party!

Acknowledgements

My life has changed a lot since I published my last book and for the better!

I have returned to full time employment and I have never been happier. I loved working with clients in my career coaching business, but I did not enjoy the relentless marketing and selling necessary to run a successful business.

In short, I totally burned out and now that I am working for someone else again, I have way more time to write and have fun!

This is the exact opposite of what I imagined when I started my business, but I am so grateful for the opportunities to live and learn and explore different paths.

I am writing every day now and my creativity is flowing as it was pre-pandemic. I am publishing stories on Kindle Vella, which is a serial reading platform, and turning those stories into books, like the one you have in your hands now.

And the best news is that I still get to stay home all day with my furry assistants, Benny and Moose. Sadly, we lost my precious Daisy in July 2021, but we gained a new goofball in Moose in February 2022. He and Benny are best friends and watching them cuddle all day fills my heart.

My husband, Jim, has been extraordinarily patient with me and my constant career flip flops over the past few years and always believes in me as I chase my dreams.

My son, Nick, is still creating more book covers for me and continues to be my biggest supporter and a firm believer in my ability to achieve big things. I am so unbelievably happy for Nick, now that he is a successful professional designer, living and working in Chicago. He's the ultimate creative partner, and a loving, inspiring source of pride and joy.

My stepdaughter, Jaime, reads all my books and celebrates with me every time I achieve a new milestone! She's graduating from law school this spring and starting a great new job in the fall. We are all so proud of her and excited for her. And just maybe there will now be some lawyers in my stories.

I am very grateful for this time in my life and I feel the best is yet to come for me professionally and personally.

As always, a special thank you to my readers, reviewers, and all of the many people who have reached out to tell me that my stories have made them laugh, cry and become absorbed in fantasy and romance.

I think of you when I am writing, and I thank you for your love and support.

About the Author

Carol Maloney Scott, author of women's humorous fiction, is a frazzled wife, proud mom and stepmom, and wiener dog fanatic.

She is a lover of donuts, and a hater of mornings. After unearthing a childhood passion for telling stories, she can once again be seen carrying around a notebook and staring into space.

Her stories are witty, fresh, and real—just like life.

Join her on "The Edge" for giveaways, cover reveals, excerpts, contests and members-only content at:

https://linktr.ee/cmscottauthor

Please check out her social media sites and say hello!

Website

Goodreads

Facebook

Pinterest

Made in United States
Troutdale, OR
08/01/2025